"We're Worlds Apart, Nick," Julia Told Him.

"A year from now, the business deal won't even be an issue. I'm talking about lifetime differences. You have your future mapped out and know what you want, and it's definitely not what I want in any man I get deeply involved with," she replied, her insides clenched. Why was she so certain she wanted to toss his offer aside as if it were nothing?

She traced her finger through the hair on his chest.

"See what you do to me with just the slightest touch?" he asked, reaching for her.

She didn't think about his offer or the future then. Tomorrow was for later....

Dear Reader,

Getting even is an intriguing motivation, and in writing this story I wondered—what happens when revenge clashes with love? Nick Ransome, the second Ransome son, is a man determined to get retribution as he charms Julia Holcomb, a glamorous blonde who intends to protect her family from this corporate shark. Passions run high because neither Nick nor Julia can resist the scalding attraction they feel for each other, and affection and vengeance become a volatile mix. Steamy kisses and seduction threaten to send Julia's world crashing into pieces. Can she protect her heart and her family from Nick? Or is Nick in as great a danger himself? Will Julia's love not only vanquish Nick's revenge, but take his heart, as well?

Enter the world of the Ransomes, where handsome, strong-willed Nick meets his match in tenderhearted, beautiful Julia, and see who wins in this blazing duel between a hot-blooded, revengeful man and a determined, loving woman. Revenge versus love, both old as time and fascinating motivators.

Sara Orwig

SARA ORWIG

REVENGE OF THE SECOND SON

Published by Silhouette Books
America's Publisher of Contemporary Romance

SILHOUETTE BOOKS

ISBN-13: 978-0-373-76757-1
ISBN-10:   0-373-76757-9

REVENGE OF THE SECOND SON

Copyright © 2006 by Sara Orwig

Visit Silhouette Books at www.eHarlequin.com

Printed in U.S.A.

SARA ORWIG

lives in Oklahoma. She has a patient husband who will take her on research trips anywhere, from big cities to old forts. She is an avid collector of Western history books. With a master's degree in English, Sara has written historical romance, mainstream fiction and contemporary romance. Books are beloved treasures that take Sara to magical worlds, and she loves both reading and writing them.

With many thanks to Melissa Jeglinski,
to Jessica Alvarez and to Maureen Walters.

One

"Time for the kill," Nick Ransome whispered to himself. Anticipation made him eager for his dinner meeting with a corporate rival he had worked years to smash.

Steering his sleek black sports car from busy Dallas traffic into the restaurant parking lot, Nick raced toward a space along a line of cars. It was still hot in the early July evening, and waves of heat shimmered up from the pavement. Suddenly, a brown shaggy dog emerged from the row of parked cars and trotted in front of Nick's car.

A woman followed, rushing toward Nick and waving her arms.

Swearing, Nick slammed on his brakes. Tires screeched when his car skidded to a stop within a foot of the female while the aged dog ambled across the drive and disappeared behind a purple crepe myrtle bush.

Nick's annoyance melted into appreciation. Dressed in knee-length, sleeveless black, the woman was a gorgeous blonde with wide blue eyes. When she walked around to the driver's side of his car, Nick watched the sway of her hips while his pulse accelerated. With interest, he lowered his window.

"I'm sorry if I startled you, but I didn't want the dog run over," she said, leaning down to talk to him. Her voice was low, as appealing as the rest of her.

"Don't worry about it. I'm happy to stop for a beautiful woman anytime."

"Thank you." She laughed, revealing even white teeth and a warm, enticing smile that jumped his pulse. Her full, rosy lips made him wonder what it would be like to kiss her. When she waved her hands, he saw there was no wedding ring. "The dog looks old, and I imagine he's deaf," she continued. "I don't think he heard your car. As long as you avoided hitting him, I'm happy."

"Anything to oblige, but you ought to take care. The next person might not stop in time."

One eyebrow arched, and her eyes twinkled. "I doubt if the next person will be driving as fast. You're a man in a hurry."

"I'm meeting people. Just in case you hurt something when you stepped in front of my car, if you'll give me your phone number, I'll check on you later," he offered with a smile.

"You're coming on to me with the same speed you drive," she remarked.

"Not really. If you want to see coming on to you fast, you give me your phone number. Or go to dinner with me tomorrow night."

When she laughed again, he smiled, but he was curious about her answer. His pulse quickened at the thought of dinner with her. She was stunning with flawless skin and enormous, thickly lashed blue eyes.

She placed both hands on his open window and leaned closer until she was only inches away. "I'm not injured. I'm not giving you my phone number. Although I'm tempted, I'm not going to dinner with you," she said in a deep-throated, sexy drawl that sent his temperature soaring. She was inches away, flirting with him, and her mouth looked enticing.

A car drove up behind him, and she stepped back.

"You're blocking traffic," she said in a breathless voice.

"You're meeting a man for dinner, aren't you?" he asked, not caring that he held up a car behind him.

"Yes," she replied. "A man I love very much." She turned and walked away as the waiting car honked. Nick watched the sway of her hips and then took his foot off the brake and drove to a parking space.

"You may love him, but you flirted with me," Nick said quietly to no one. Nick arched an eyebrow and wondered about her.

By the time he had reached the entrance, she had disappeared inside. He wanted her name. She was dining with a man tonight, but if she wasn't married or engaged, then that was no hurdle to getting to know her. She couldn't be truly in love and act like she had. Unless the man she loved was her father. The last possibility made Nick smile.

Nick vowed he would get to know her. He laughed at himself. Why bother? Texas was filled with beautiful, sexy, interesting women. Still, when the maître d' greeted him and turned to lead him to his table, Nick scanned the room for sight of her.

"Your party is waiting, Mr. Ransome," Darrell said, threading his way across the room. Nick glanced again at well-dressed people seated at tables, adorned with white linen cloths, candles and roses in crystal vases, in one of Dallas's finest steak houses. A piano player's soft, background music was a complement to the inviting ambience. It was Wednesday, the first week of July—Nick decided it had been a very good way to start the evening.

Darrell stepped out of the way, motioning Nick to a table with three people. Both men stood, but Nick's gaze went to the blonde who remained seated and gazed back impassively.

His pulse jumped and for the second time in the past fifteen minutes, she gave him another jolt. If, in turn, his identity surprised her, she hid it well. And he knew any dinner involving just the two of them was off. His interest in her cooled to a glacial temperature.

Distaste and dull anger made Nick's throat tight as he shook hands with Rufus Holcomb, CEO of Holcomb Drilling. The white-haired man gave Nick a firm handshake and Nick gazed into calculating blue eyes beneath shaggy white brows. The old man was shrewd, scheming and stubborn; Nick could feel the invisible tangle of wills as he greeted Rufus, their smiles belying what he knew each of them felt.

"Rufus, I've been looking forward to this," Nick said, wondering why Rufus had wanted to meet for dinner.

"I can imagine," Rufus answered dryly and turned to the blonde. "Julia, this is the infamous Nick Ransome," he said. "Nick, meet my granddaughter, Julia Holcomb."

She extended her hand and smiled coolly. "We've met," she said, gazing steadfastly at Nick as she gave him a firm handshake. The moment he clasped her slender hand in his, his pulse jumped another notch and he couldn't resist a glance at her full, pouty lips.

"So we have. Protector of dogs and grandfathers," he said, releasing her hand and turning to a stocky blond man, shaking hands perfunctorily with Ransome Energy's senior vice president of marketing and his lifelong friend, Tyler Wade.

When the three men sat, the waiter appeared to take drink orders. As soon as the waiter left, Rufus glanced at Nick and Julia. "So where and how did you two meet, since it had to have been after six this evening? And what's this about protecting dogs?"

"Mr. Ransome is a fast driver and a stray wandered in front of his car tonight in the parking lot," Julia said, watching Nick. The minute their gazes locked, he inhaled and his pulse jumped. "I imagine Mr. Ransome is fast in many things he does. Am I right?"

Nick could feel the friction that he had always experienced around Rufus extend to Julia, only it was different. Julia was a desirable woman and a challenge that he couldn't ignore. "I would never tell a beautiful woman that she's wrong," Nick said smoothly, turning to Rufus. "You're a scoundrel, Rufus, bringing your granddaughter, because you're fully aware that all she has to do is bat her big blue eyes and she would tempt any man to give away the farm."

Nick knew his sexist remark would make both Holcombs bristle, particularly since Rufus was always ready to fight. Nick wondered what it was about Julia that made him want to needle her.

"Julia is a vice president in our accounting department. As you'll soon see, she's an excellent employee to have at my side."

"Thank you, Granddad. I doubt if Mr. Ransome will share your opinion or be in a position to know what kind of employee I am," she said, smiling at Nick. But it was another chilly smile that conveyed no friendliness, and nothing like the irresistible, warm smiles she had flashed when they had been in the parking lot. Her blond hair was pulled behind her head and tied with a black scarf; he wondered how she would look if it were unfastened and loose over her shoulders.

"I'm sure your granddad is correct," Nick replied. His emotions warred between competing with her and wanting to take her out and get to know her.

They paused when the sommelier appeared to uncork a bottle of wine, pour some for Nick's approval and then fill the wineglasses. As soon as he left them, Rufus picked up his menu. "I'm starving and it's been a long day. Actually, I usually eat almost two hours earlier, so let's get some food on the table."

"Fine," Nick answered, knowing what he wanted because of his familiarity with the menu. He was eager to get on with the dinner that he expected would accomplish nothing except antagonize both the old man and his granddaughter further.

There was a brief discussion of various selections before the waiter appeared to tell them about the specials and then to take orders.

"I know you've got two splendid quarter horses you race out at that ranch of yours," Rufus said. "How're they doing this season?"

"Still winning," Nick answered.

"Black Lightning won just last Saturday," Julia said.

"You go to the races?" Nick asked her.

"No. I keep up with your horses. I think it's wise to know your competitors," she said.

"What else do I do that you keep up with?" he asked, smiling at her.

"You've been very successful. Your company has tripled in size in the past five years. You recently signed a deal to drill in Russia."

"You do know about us," Nick said, surprised. Their green salads came and conversation went back to quarter horses and breeding stock. All the time they talked, whenever Nick and Julia's gazes met, he could feel electricity crackle between them. To his consternation, he acknowledged to himself that it took his breath just to look at her. Her flawless skin looked silky and soft. He wanted to sink his fingers in her golden hair. Several times, he jerked his thoughts back to the conversation when they drifted to erotic images of her.

Over thick, juicy steaks, their conversation went from Nick's horses to Rufus's hobby of sailing.

"You could retire, Rufus, and spend all your time sailing since you enjoy it so much," Nick remarked.

Rufus's mouth curled in a wolfish grin and he shook his head. "And let you steal my company? I don't think so. No, I'll continue like I am. Julia's as good a sailor as I am. With her help, I expect to win the upcoming race, just as we intend to block you in a buyout."

"So sailing is in your blood, too," Nick said to her, ignoring Rufus's remarks about business.

"Granddad's been taking me sailing since I was five years old."

"She's got her own sailboat and it's a real beauty," Rufus said.

"What's the name of your boat?" Nick asked. "I may have to come watch you race."

"Granddad is the one racing. I'll be his crew," she replied, ignoring Nick's question.

Their conversation remained neutral until coffee was served.

"Do you really think that our lawyers can sit down together Friday and hash out anything?" Julia asked, toying with her Bavarian apple tart dessert. "We don't see any point in having them meet," she added, gazing at Nick. Grudgingly, he had to admire her poise, she looked and sounded as if she had the upper hand in this struggle.

"If they meet, we might find common ground. And all of you can listen to my offer," Nick replied.

"You can keep your so-called offer," Rufus snapped. "You're trying to rob me of Holcomb Drilling."

"I have no intention of stealing your company," Nick said. "The offer we're going to bring to the table will be generous, cover your debts and give you an opportunity to retire and enjoy life."

"Granddad isn't ready to retire," Julia remarked.

"Indeed, I'm not! Whatever your offer is, I'm turning it down. You might as well know that right now, Nick. As a matter of fact, you back off, damn quick, or I'll ruin you in every way. You'll regret going after Holcomb."

Hanging on to his temper, Nick sipped his water, setting down his glass. "Don't threaten me, Rufus," he remarked quietly. "I'm not a young, green rookie just starting in business anymore."

"Doesn't matter. You back off if you know what's good for you."

"Frankly, I want what you have and you've had some setbacks that have dealt Holcomb Drilling financial blows. If I don't step in and take over, someone else will. It's inevitable."

"It's no such thing," Julia answered quietly, and Nick met her gaze. She could play poker and not give anything away, he realized. She looked as impassive as if she were discussing the weather. Her granddad was not dealing as well with the conversation, Rufus's face had reddened and his fists were clenched. "Don't come after our company," she said quietly. "It won't be in your best interests if you do."

"So you, too, are threatening me," Nick remarked, banking his anger but impressed by her confidence. He saw the flash of fire in the depths of her eyes. Would she play as dirty as her deceased father had and her granddad? "Is this why you wanted to get together—to threaten me?"

Nick leaned toward her. "You want a fight, you'll get a fight," he said quietly. When she drew a deep breath, her breasts pushed against the black fabric of her dress. Nick let his gaze roam down and then up.

"You'll know you've been in a battle, too, Mr. Ransome," she stated flatly. "Granddad," Julia said, placing her hand over his, "let's go. I don't think Mr. Ransome has any intention of cooperating or listening. There's no need in dragging out the evening." She stood and all the men came to their feet.

She looked up at Nick. "You'll never acquire anything from us," she said firmly. "You should spend your time taking care of what you have. And watching where you're going."

He was caught and held by invisible bonds, gazing back down at her and feeling the air between them crackle. He struggled to hang on to his temper, yet at the same time attraction burned hot and intense. She was desirable, beautiful and defiant and the competitor in him wanted to best her, while the healthy male that he was wanted her naked in his arms.

"Admit it, Mr. Ransome," Julia said. "Your motive is revenge for times in the past when Granddad has bested you. Revenge is what this is about."

"This will be a lucrative deal for all concerned," Nick replied, keeping calm. "You'll get rid of a lot of debt."

"We'll manage our company," Julia replied smoothly, turning to Tyler. "I'm glad to have met you."

Looping her arm through her grandfather's, she turned to Nick. "I guess if I hadn't stepped in front of you, you would have run right over that poor old dog. Manners force me to thank you for dinner, but it's been less than pleasant. You may want revenge for imagined wrongs, but you're not going to get it," she added. "Back off, or you'll regret it."

Taking her grandfather's arm, Julia started to walk away. Nick inhaled and his gaze drifted down over her, watching the sexy sway of her hips, looking at her long, shapely legs. He wanted her in an explosive way, wishing he could yank her into his embrace and kiss her into submission. At the same time, he was annoyed with himself.

He watched her walk across the restaurant until she was out of sight. Beside him, Tyler gave a long, low whistle. "She's a pistol! Wow! And a real chip off the old block. I knew the old man was grooming her to take over, but I didn't expect it this much and this soon, or his heir to be red-hot sexy and drop-dead gorgeous."

Nick turned to his vice president. "I think she brings out the Neanderthal in me," he said, and Tyler gave a dry laugh.

"She'd bring it out in any man who's not dead. Whew! She's feisty and maybe as underhanded as the rest of her family. She openly threatened you."

"That will make this all the more interesting. Too bad she's a Holcomb. Otherwise…" he let his voice trail away as he thought about Julia. "Let's have coffee," Nick said, sitting and facing Tyler. "Tell me again—we've got this takeover nailed, don't we?"

"Yes, we do," Tyler said, his gray eyes flashing with satisfaction. He poured more wine for himself and offered some to Nick, who shook his head.

"Make sure there aren't any hitches. Rufus has killer instincts and he doesn't draw the line at doing something illegal."

"As long as you live, you'll think it was one of their minions who ran you off the road back in your early days."

"I know damn well it was, but there was no way to prove it in court. None. My word against them, and they would have had an alibi."

"If that's the case, be careful now. We're going for his throat."

"I'm not a kid now. I'm not worried about Rufus or Julia and her threats. More than ever, I want to destroy Holcomb and get revenge for my family."

"Plus acquiring some real jewels," Tyler declared, taking a long drink of wine. "Rufus's sister, Helena, lives in Paris. Her health is failing and she has a nurse and companion, as well as a staff to take care of her condo. I flew over there myself to see her. She never wants to come back here."

"That surprises me," Nick said.

"She's older than Rufus and thinks it's high time he retired while he still has his health. She has definite ideas and it sounds as if the two haven't gotten along from the day Rufus was born."

"Julia isn't close to her aunt?"

"No. Helena doesn't think Julia should be at Holcomb. Helena's opinion is that Julia should be home making babies."

The image that popped into Nick's mind temporarily wiped out hearing anything else that Tyler was telling him. Julia in bed. Nick's temperature soared, and he tried to pull his thoughts back to Tyler and concentrate on his vice president's conversation. Nick wiped his damp brow and stared at Tyler.

"We own every dime's worth of Holcomb stock Helena possessed. You are now the major stockholder."

"Are there any other relatives holding stock besides Julia and Rufus?"

"No. In addition to Rufus's sister, Julia and Rufus are the only ones left. They only have each other," Tyler exclaimed with eagerness. "Julia's parents were killed in a plane crash three years ago. Between the Holcomb stocks and the bank, you've got 'em."

Nick thought about the bank he had just purchased and the Holcomb mortgages he had acquired. "We can call those mortgages in whenever we want," he said. "His family and ours have battled over horses and oil. It's time to take Miss Julia Holcomb and her grandfather out of the picture. She'll make a lot of money and so will Rufus. We're not robbing them."

A cell phone rang and Nick retrieved it from his pocket, talking softly and listening to his friend, Meredith Cates, while Tyler poured another glass of wine for himself.

"Sorry, Meredith. I'm tied up this weekend." Nick listened while she fussed.

"I can't change my plans. I'll get back with you," he said and switched off his phone.

"Another woman bites the dust," Tyler said. "You go through them like lightning. Has there ever been one you couldn't seduce?"

Nick smiled. "I'm sure there has," he answered easily. "Although I can't remember her," he added, and they both laughed.

Tyler sipped his drink and gazed at his friend. "All right," Nick said. "What's up?"

"It's after hours now, Nick. Business over."

Nick nodded. "Right. I think I should do Gina a favor and drive you home."

"Nope. I'm sober enough. I'll tell you what—I want that year-old sorrel of yours—"

"Standing Tall? He's still not for sale," Nick replied firmly. "But you have an eye for horseflesh. He's going to win me a bunch of races."

"You like my new Ferrari, don't you?"

"Yes, but I don't want to swap my horse for your car. I can buy a car. The horse takes breeding and luck."

"You might not have to have to swap your horse. You might get both if you're willing to take a risk."

Nick drank the last of his coffee and set down his cup, his curiosity growing. "So what's on your not-too-sober mind, Tyler?"

"Let me name a woman. If you can seduce her within the next two weeks, the car is yours. If you can't, the horse is mine."

Nick laughed. "You've lost it!"

"Listen to me. I'll pick someone likely—she has to be under thirty, healthy, single, a knockout, unattached and a woman of my choice."

"You're nuts. You've had enough wine. Let's go," Nick said and stood. "We've done a lot of crazy things, Ty. This is one you're not talking me into."

"Since when do you balk at seduction of a beautiful woman?" Tyler said, standing and walking out beside Nick. "Scared to risk your horse? You might get my Ferrari."

Thinking about the prize car, Nick glanced at his friend. "You'd really bet your car?"

"Yes, I will. I want that horse. I think I can name a woman you can't seduce."

"Maybe. Maybe not."

"C'mon, Nick. It'll make life interesting. Matter of fact,"

Tyler said, getting a brisk, businesslike tone back in his voice, "here's your chance to make your revenge really sweet. Miss Julia Holcomb."

"To hell with that one," Nick said.

"Scared of her? That would be the ultimate revenge, Nick. Absolute. I know your negative answer is not because she isn't attractive enough. Sparks were flying between the two of you tonight."

"Forget it, Ty. I'm not eighteen anymore, and you're not talking me into something crazy like you used to do."

Tyler kicked a small rock as they crossed the parking lot. "There goes my horse."

Nick laughed. "C'mon. I'll take you home and Gina can bring you back tomorrow to pick up your car."

As they crossed the parking lot Nick remembered Julia and their encounter. How long was it going to take him to forget her? Or his pulse to stop jumping at the mere thought of her? Seduce Julia? Just the suggestion made his breath catch. But he wasn't getting into a crazy bet with Tyler, even though it would be both a challenge and sweet revenge to seduce her.

After depositing Tyler at his house, Nick headed to his condo. While he drove, he thought about dinner and his fiery exchanges with Julia Holcomb, the sparks he could feel every time he locked gazes with her.

Beautiful, sexy, pure poison because of her family. He knew she viewed him as a monster.

I guess if I hadn't stepped in front of you, you would have run right over that poor old dog. As her words rang in his ears, Nick clamped his jaw shut. He might be ruthless at work, but he didn't run down helpless animals. He knew she'd said it to aggravate him, and his annoyance increased that she'd succeeded.

Nick drove to his condo that was the entire top floor of a twenty-story building. He moved around in the dark, enjoying the lights of the city, still unable to keep memories of Julia from tormenting him. He stood by the window and looked down on the sparkling city lights that sprawled in all directions. She was somewhere out there, probably in bed asleep. That thought made him groan, and he turned away, switching on lights as he shed clothes. He wished he were out on his ranch where he could go for night ride. Restless, he crossed to his desk and pulled out a ledger to think about work and get his mind off big blue eyes, long legs and the fiery tension between him and Julia Holcomb.

It was after three in the morning before he fell asleep, but within thirty minutes, the ringing of his phone awakened him. Immediately alert, Nick stretched out a long arm and picked up the receiver. His first thought was that something might have happened to his dad, whose health wasn't the greatest.

"Nick."

He heard Tyler's voice. "Is Dad okay?"

"Yeah, sure. Sorry. I'm not calling about your family."

Relief swamped Nick and he flopped down in bed again. "That's good. What are you calling about?"

"There was an explosion on one of our rigs in the Gulf. Now there's a fire."

"Dammit!" Nick swung out of bed. A tight knot of anger curled in his stomach. "Was anyone hurt?"

"Two men have been evacuated to a burn center."

"Get the helicopter to meet me in Galveston. I can be there within the hour," Nick said, grabbing jeans.

"Just hold tight and I'll keep you posted. You don't have to be out there fighting the fire. That'll just worry your dad more. You're going to have to break the news to him because he's going to hear it in the morning anyway."

"Tyler, you find out exactly what happened, down to the tiniest detail," Nick said, anger burning him. "If there is anything that points to the Holcombs, I'm going to sell off that company of his bit by bit and wreck what I can't sell."

"I'll get back with you."

"I'll call Dad in the morning. He doesn't get up as early as he used to. The more casual I can be about it, the less concerned he'll be. Maybe by that time, you'll know more."

"I'll keep you posted."

Nick replaced the receiver, staring at the phone speculatively. He stepped out of bed, because sleeping again was impossible. Remembering clearly Julia's and Rufus's threats, Nick doubled his fists. Had she been behind the destruction? Or had her grandfather?

At eight o'clock the next morning, Nick's intercom buzzed and he listened to his secretary's voice. "Julia Holcomb is on the phone and would like to see you today, if possible. Your calendar is clear in an hour and at two this afternoon."

Surprised, he stared across his office and seethed with anger.

"I'll see her in an hour," he said flatly, his mind racing over what he wanted to do while he was curious about what she intended. He picked up a remote, switched on the news on the flat-panel television mounted on a wall across the room, and looked at images of what had been a productive Ransome oil rig only twenty-four hours earlier.

He stared while his anger climbed. Switching off the television, he tossed down the remote, picked up his phone and dialed Tyler's cell number. In seconds, Tyler answered, static crackling.

"Any more news?" Nick asked.

"The fire expert is looking into the cause."

"Remember that offer of a bet? Is it still on?"

"Bet?" Tyler sounded perplexed momentarily. "Ah, the horse and the car."

"You're on," Nick snapped. "If the Holcombs want a fight, they'll get a fight. If I seduce Julia within two weeks, I win your prize car."

"And if you don't, I want your horse," Tyler replied, his voice fading.

"Keep me posted."

"What? I'm losing you, Nick."

Nick replaced the receiver and stared at the door, not seeing his office, but remembering Julia Holcomb's blue eyes, her long legs. Revenge would be sweet. Seduction would be just the beginning.

As his appointment with Julia Holcomb approached, Nick glanced around, hoping that his office was bigger, finer and more intimidating than her own. Immediately, he had to laugh at himself. Never in his life had he felt that way with anyone, much less someone he was going to destroy.

He looked at the walnut paneling, the thick oriental carpet in muted colors, the oversized, polished mahogany table that served as his desk and brown leather furniture. The walls of his office held original oils by famous painters, art acquired on his trips to Europe. He was located on the eighteenth floor of the Ransome Building in downtown Dallas. He knew Holcomb Drilling was in a ten-story, suburban brick building that had been built about twenty years earlier to replace the old offices in downtown Dallas.

The intercom buzzed, and his secretary announced Julia's arrival.

As the door closed behind Julia, he rose to his feet. She was as beautiful as he remembered. He hoped his features were as impassive as hers, but he couldn't resist an appreciative head-to-toe glance. Taking in her tailored black suit and blouse, her blond hair coiled and pinned on her head, he wanted to tangle his fingers in that neat hairdo and watch those silky locks fall.

"Good morning," he said, smiling at her. "Welcome to the wolf's den."

Two

"Good morning. I'm surprised you admit it," Julia said, smiling as she crossed the room and extended her hand to shake Nick's.

"Why wouldn't I think this is a good morning?" he asked, something flashing in the depths of his dark eyes.

"Since I'm paying a call," she answered.

In a long-legged easy stride, Nick came around from behind his desk. His charcoal suit added to his dark, handsome looks which she tried to avoid thinking about as much as she tried to ignore her excitement at the sight of him. She loathed dealing with Nick and beneath what she hoped was a cool, collected facade, she fought a rising panic over what Nick was about to do to her grandfather and what she could not stop.

When she shook hands with him, his fingers closed around hers, warm and firm, in a contact that sizzled to her toes. How could she be so physically drawn to him when emotionally she viewed him as a ruthless competitor? She withdrew her hand swiftly.

"Won't you be seated," he said, motioning her to a leather chair. He pulled another chair around to face her and sat only a few feet away. His brown eyes bore into her and she tried to remain cool.

She crossed her legs and noticed his gaze drifting down to her ankles. Just a look from him made her tingle. She was accustomed to having control of most aspects of her life and she was chagrined to discover her reaction to Nick Ransome today was as volatile as her response during the first few minutes in the restaurant parking lot.

"I know you won't make this easy for me," she said.

"I'm damned astounded you're here," he admitted with a frankness that took her by surprise.

Unable to avoid noticing how thickly lashed his dark eyes were, she stared back at him. "I thought we ought to get on better footing than we were last night."

"I find that also amazing," he added. He looked relaxed, sitting in the chair, one ankle on his knee, but she had a feeling that he was holding back fury. His dark brown eyes sparked with fire. His curly, dark brown hair softened his features slightly.

"I know we parted on a bad note last night—"

"That's rather an understatement."

"I thought perhaps I should try again to persuade you to let go your intentions to acquire Holcomb Drilling."

"My objectives have been reinforced since dinner."

"Your hostility has grown," she said, wondering about his barely banked fury. "Maybe there's no point in this visit."

"Are you aware that one of our rigs burned in the night?"

"No, I didn't know that." She didn't try to hide her surprise and then guessed the reason for his smoldering anger. "That's what you've been referring to—"

"An explosion of an unknown origin caused the fire." His words were clipped and his eyes blazed with anger.

"You're blaming us?"

"Did Rufus hire someone to do it?" Nick cut in with a voice as cold as ice.

"No!" she exclaimed, furious that he would jump to conclusions without proof. "Granddad would never stoop to something like that. Or risk the lives of people who have nothing to do with the fight between the two of you. Never!"

"I'm afraid it'll take more than your denial to convince me," Nick said in what she thought was an annoying stubbornness to lay blame on her family.

"If there was an explosion or fire since we were together last night, aren't you being premature in jumping to conclusions about the cause?" she asked. "I think it often takes time to discover what starts a fire."

Something flickered in the depths of his dark eyes. "You're right, of course," he said pleasantly, his anger vanishing as if she had waved a magic wand. "Until I hear from the arson experts, I'll hold my judgment about the cause."

"That's the only sensible thing to do," she replied.

"In the meantime, what brings you to my office?" he asked in a pleasant tone, ignoring her sarcasm.

He smiled and waited. She gazed back steadfastly, her anger with him rising and becoming a tight, knot inside. She didn't trust his friendliness for a second. He had turned it on like switching on a light, and the warmth in his voice couldn't conceal the fiery anger in his eyes. Determined to not let him know how disturbed she felt, she concentrated on being civil and hiding her fury.

"I want to meet with you again, informally as we did last night, and see what we can work out," she replied, hoping she sounded as relaxed and friendly as he had. "We both have old companies that were family-owned for many years. There aren't many of those around any longer. I want to keep our company intact as long as Granddad is living. This company has been his whole life."

"Perhaps your granddad shouldn't have spread himself so thin," Nick remarked dryly.

Banking her annoyance, she nodded. "Maybe, if you're willing to try, we can work something out that will be to your satisfaction and ours. You surely will be reasonable enough to discuss the matter informally before the lawyers take charge tomorrow."

She hoped she looked and sounded amiable, far from how she felt. She loved her granddad and if the company were taken from him, she was afraid it would be the end of him. He had devoted his life to it and now to see it in precarious straits kept her sleepless at night. The problem was compounded by the fact that it was Nick who was after Holcomb Drilling. The Ransomes and Holcombs were old enemies, forever business competitors. She stared into Nick's brown eyes; his bland gaze belied the chemistry between them. Her breath caught. She couldn't move or speak or think, and he was doing nothing except look at her. She was caught and held, her heart pounding loudly enough that she wondered if he could hear it. She hated her reaction, to him, yet she couldn't prevent it.

"All right," he agreed. "We'll keep it informal. You and your granddad like boats and the water. I have a twenty-footer, give or take a few feet, that sleeps six. It's docked in Galveston Bay. We can fly down there and spend the weekend on the water."

Startled, she stared at him while she mulled his offer. "A weekend together? I had dinner in mind."

He shrugged. "You wanted a casual, friendly meeting. A weekend on the water—we can stay out of each other's way or talk, whatever we want to do. The weekend would be casual— and we'll get to know each other and what each one of us wants," he said pleasantly.

Her mind raced. She had never expected several days with Nick Ransome. Yet this might give her the chance to win him over and talk him into leaving Holcomb Drilling untouched. The more she thought about it, the more she liked the idea. "What if I come without Granddad?" she asked, "I'd like to be able to speak freely without worrying him."

"Fine," Nick said, something again flickering in the depths of his eyes. "I think the weather is supposed to be good, so we should have a calm time."

"The two of us together—a 'calm' time? I don't think it's possible."

He gave her a taunting, crooked smile. "Then if not calm, interesting."

"If we're not at each other's throats, it'll be a smashing success," she said. He touched the corner of her mouth, she tingled from the contact.

"There would be only one reason for me to be 'at your throat,'" he drawled in a husky voice.

"Now you're flirting," she accused.

"Don't sound so surprised. You're a beautiful woman."

"I rather distrust your motives for turning on your charm."

"I meant what I said," he insisted.

"Very well. A weekend on the water," she said, not feeling the relief and satisfaction she had expected to feel if he agreed to getting together. "Since we're going to talk more about the company, can we postpone tomorrow's meeting and let our lawyers get together next week?"

"It's fine with me to move the meeting. Make it a week from Friday," Nick replied, flashing her a smile that curled her toes. His white teeth were a contrast with his dark skin; creases bracketed his mouth and heightened his appeal. "I'll pick you up tomorrow about four and we can fly to Galveston," he said, getting up to go around his desk for pen and paper. "Give me your address."

"Write out where to meet you at the dock. I don't mind the drive to Galveston and I have an errand to run on the way," she said, not wanting to fly with him. She watched his well-shaped hands as he wrote an address. She stood and he moved beside her to show her what he had written.

He stood close enough that his shoulder and arm brushed against her. She could detect his enticing aftershave, feel the warmth from his body. Her drumming pulse was impossible to control.

There was no denying the reaction she had to Nick. Was she making a wise move to spend the weekend on Nick's boat—just the two of them, plus his crew in the background? Yet it was the only way she could see to try to win Nick's friendship so that he would at least listen to reason when they were ready to negotiate.

As it stood now, she and Nick were at loggerheads, and that would do nothing to win Nick Ransome over to doing what she wanted.

On the other hand, to be shut away with Nick for the weekend on a boat sent her heart racing into overdrive. She reassured herself that she and Nick wouldn't really be alone, and they would be together only for the weekend.

As Nick gave her directions, she struggled to listen. He turned to face her, and they stood only inches apart.

"If you prefer, I'll send a car to pick you up tomorrow—about four and you can still do your errands."

"Thanks, but I'll drive myself," she replied, and one corner of his mouth lifted in a wicked grin.

"Scared to leave transportation behind?" he asked.

"Of course not, or I wouldn't have suggested coming by myself," she replied, trying to ignore the butterflies fluttering in her stomach. Taking the directions from his hand, she picked up her purse and headed for the door. Suddenly he was there in front of her, reaching around her. Instead of opening the door, he stepped closer and blocked her with his hand on the knob, his arm a barrier. She turned to look up at him.

"So is it going to be all business this weekend?" he asked in a husky, seductive voice that created a honeyed warmth in her.

"Probably not," she replied breathlessly, wishing she could wrap him around her little finger and get what she wanted from him. Nick leaned closer and his gaze lowered to her mouth.

Her lips parted, tingling, but she moved around him and placed her hand over his on the knob. The instant she touched him, another fiery current simmered from her fingers to her toes.

She looked up at him. "I need to open the door."

With a smile, he swung the door wide and then he followed her into the reception area. "Tomorrow afternoon about five or six."

"Fine," she said, glancing over her shoulder at him. At the outer door, she looked back to find him still watching her. The minute she was in the hallway, her smile vanished. "What have I done?" she asked herself as she stepped into the empty elevator. "The only thing you could do," she answered herself, butterflies still fluttering in her stomach, her palms sweaty from spending the past few minutes with Nick.

No man had ever disturbed her the way Nick had and that worried her most of all because she was usually in control of her responses.

All the rest of the day and far into the night, she weighed the pros and cons of spending a weekend with him. Yet she had to do something to try to get a satisfactory settlement, or even better, get Nick to back off and leave Holcomb Drilling unscathed.

The next afternoon, as she drove over the arching causeway to Galveston and looked below at sparkling blue water, she asked herself the same question worrying her constantly since leaving his office. Would this weekend help save Holcomb Drilling?

Could she resist Nick's sex appeal? She reminded herself that all she had to do was remember what he intended to do to her heritage and future.

She shook her shoulders as if she banished a problem. How easy it was to think his appeal diminished when she was miles away from him!

"Be polite, professional," she reminded herself, glancing at the rearview mirror. She wanted something from him and there was no hope of getting it if she exposed her fury.

In minutes she parked at the Galveston Yacht Club. She slipped her backpack and her purse over her shoulder and picked up her briefcase. Taking a deep breath as if going into a battle, she circled the yacht club and strolled down to the wharf to look for the slip with his boat. She spotted him in cutoffs, a T-shirt and wraparound sunglasses. He and another man were in a motorboat. When Nick saw her, he sprang to the dock and came striding forward to meet her.

It was warm and she'd worn cutoffs, a cotton shirt, deck shoes and sunglasses and she suspected that behind his dark glasses, he was giving her a quick, thorough assessment. An appraisal that she gave him in return while her pulse thudded. His T-shirt molded sculpted muscles, the short sleeves stretched by thick biceps. His chest tapered to a narrow waist, flat stomach and well-muscled legs. The cutoffs were brief and tight. She should have guessed that beneath those elegant suits he wore, he had muscles.

The same mixture of attraction and dislike gripped her. She hated his intentions to destroy her family's business but, as a woman, she responded eagerly to Nick.

"You really intend to work," he said, taking her briefcase from her.

"Certainly. That's the whole point of getting together this weekend."

"I thought my personality enticed you."

She had to laugh at him. "With the lifelong differences between us? I don't think so."

"When you weren't here half an hour ago, I thought you'd changed your mind about sailing with me," he said.

"No. Just a slight delay," she said, startled that he guessed that she'd almost canceled the weekend. Duty urged her to do what she could and spend time with him, so she was going to follow her conscience.

"Great," he said, taking her arm. He waved her briefcase slightly. "I'll make a bargain with you. In the interest of getting acquainted and laying some groundwork for keeping things civil between us, no business discussions until twenty-four hours from now. That way, we'll have a pleasant weekend, get acquainted and get down to the nuts and bolts maybe tomorrow this time. How's that for a deal?"

"Fine with me," she said, looking into his unfathomable brown eyes and wondering what was behind his suggestion. Was he laying the groundwork for seduction? The mere speculation thrilled her in a way she hated.

"Good," Nick replied cheerfully. "Come meet my captain, Luis."

Nick jumped into the motorboat, causing it to rock slightly. He set down her briefcase, took her backpack and purse. Then his hands closed around her waist and he swung her into the boat. He lifted her easily and they gazed into each other's eyes while he held her. Her hands rested on his forearms, where she detected the flex of solid muscles. Each contact heightened her reaction to him. He held her a fraction longer than necessary and she stood with her hands on his forearms when she could have stepped away. As she looked into his brown eyes, she knew he wanted her. He released her and turned to a man standing in the boat.

"Julia, this is Luis Reyna. Luis, this is Miss Holcomb."

She greeted the tall black-haired man and then she sat in the front of the boat. She watched Nick's muscles ripple and flex as he unfastened the line and pushed away, and in seconds, they chugged slowly from the dock.

"So where are we headed? I know we're not spending the weekend in this," she said, looking at a number of yachts and sailboats at anchor.

"There's my boat, *For Ransome*," he said, pointing to the southwest.

She followed his gaze to see a large, sleek yacht. "Give or take a few feet," she said, repeating what he had told her about his boat. "It has to be over forty feet long," she said, eyeing the white yacht that had teak accents and a thin gold stripe on the hull. Nick smiled and shrugged.

When they were alongside, a man dropped a ladder over the side. Nick took her backpack and purse and scrambled up, turning to help her, leaning down to circle her waist with his arm and swing her to the deck.

This time, he released her immediately. "Julia, this is Dorian Landry. Dorian, meet my guest, Miss Holcomb."

She greeted the man and then walked away while the two men talked. Nick's luxurious yacht exceeded her family's large, comfortable sailboat, reinforcing her awareness of Nick as a powerful, formidable opponent no matter how sexy and appealing he appeared.

"Let me show you your cabin," he said, catching up with her. She followed him down a companionway to a spacious starboard cabin with a cream berth in beige and white decor.

"Want to come above while we head out? We'll travel along the coast. I'll give you the official tour of my boat later."

"Sure," she said, setting down her things, aware that in spite of the roominess, Nick dominated the cabin with his height and presence. When they went above, to her surprise, Nick took the wheel and she glanced around. "Where's Luis? And Dorian?"

"They're headed back," Nick said with a jerk of his head.

Startled, she frowned at Nick. "We're *alone?*"

"Yes. I thought that's what we agreed," he replied, looking at her and his eyes narrowing. "Changed your mind? I can take you back."

"No," she answered, questions tumbling in her mind. Could they be civil to each other through the entire weekend? Would she be able to resist his charm? Could she cope with him alone for hours on end?

"Of course not," she replied, hoping her voice sounded cool and composed and far from giving away mild panic. "I was just surprised that you didn't keep a crew on board."

"No need," he answered easily, gazing ahead as if his thoughts were more on navigating than on her. "I like handling the boat and I'm sure you don't want every minute of my time," he remarked dryly, turning to meet her gaze. Electricity sparked between them and she couldn't look away. Silence stretched, crackling with tension.

His dark chocolate, thickly lashed bedroom eyes could nail her and she wondered how much he saw. He was fit, handsome and she had to admire his drive and energy, which she wished he had directed somewhere besides at her family.

Did he know how she truly felt toward him, that the weekend was a sham? She wanted something from him and she intended to get it.

She inhaled, but she still couldn't look away. Then his cell phone rang, breaking the spell. To give him privacy, she started to leave, but Nick motioned her to remain while he listened to his call.

"No, we're not losing that property, Tyler. Go as high as you need to, but you see that we're the buyers," Nick said and then was quiet again. "I don't care. Just acquire the leases, whatever you have to pay." Another moment of silence. Wind had tangled his curly hair, and unruly locks just added to his handsome looks.

"We're losing the connection, Tyler. You've got your authority and instructions." Nick turned off the phone and set it down.

As she listened to him, descriptions materialized in her thoughts—sexy, ruthless, driven, handsome, good, bad and irresistible. His hands moved lightly over the wheel and he glanced at her. "I don't exactly see approval in your expression."

She shrugged. "I don't know enough to approve or not approve."

"Oh, yes, you do. You know my company will outbid the others no matter what price. You don't approve."

"I don't know the circumstances. I just know you like to win."

"I'd guess we're cut out of the same cloth there. I don't think you like to lose, either," he said dryly.

"I doubt if winning or losing is as all-important to me as much as it is you. There are other things that I give my efforts to."

"Is that right? So how do you like to spend your time?" he asked. His voice transformed into a lower, huskier tone that gave his question a hint of sexual innuendo.

"Get your mind off sex," she said lightly. "You know that wasn't my reference."

"I can always hope," he replied, and she smiled.

"There, that would melt the hardest heart," he said, touching the corner of her mouth. "What temptation!"

"Perhaps now you should concentrate on getting your yacht into open water."

He nodded, but his gaze remained on her. With an effort, she pulled her attention from him. Breathless, she left to get distance between them, stepping out into sunshine and fresh air, wanting to fan herself and knowing that her warmth wasn't caused by the weather. Also knowing that his brief phone conversation revealed how important winning was to him.

She moved to the railing and let the wind tangle her hair as a fine spray blew back over her. She watched gulls circling, swooping down to scoop something from the water. A jellyfish, a pale transparent blob, occasionally floated near the surface and then vanished from her sight. She thought about yesterday afternoon when she had gone to see her granddad, asking him directly if he knew anything about the fire on the Ransome oil rig.

His blue eyes had widened. "No, I don't know anything about a fire." He scowled. "Why would you think I'd know? Did Ransome or some of his people accuse us of that?"

"Nick Ransome thought we might have been the reason for the fire. As of now, the cause is unknown."

"That bastard. He'll say or do anything, just like his father."

"Forget it, Granddad. I just wanted to hear you say that we had no part in it." She had wanted to be sure, but now wished she hadn't brought up the matter.

Reassured, she looked down at the blue-green water sweeping against the yacht and hoped the fire experts learned exactly what had caused the blaze. Would Nick admit to her that he had been wrong to accuse her granddad? She doubted if he would.

She glanced over her shoulder and could see Nick inside at the wheel. They were alone on this boat for the weekend. She hoped she could hide her stormy emotions from him.

The Gulf was smooth and the breeze was cool, a perfect day that appeared peaceful and gave no hint of the turmoil churning inside her. She enjoyed the ride, but knew if she wanted to win Nick over, she wouldn't succeed by avoiding him. She wondered how many women he had brought on board that had wanted all his time and attention.

She returned to the pilothouse and when she reached his side, he stepped away slightly. "Want to take the wheel?"

"Sure," she said, taking it, aware of their hands brushing before he stepped aside. Spreading his feet, he placed his hands on his hips as he watched her.

"So you've been sailing since you were five," he commented. "Is this one of your favorite pastimes or are you doing it to be nice to your granddad?"

"I enjoy sailing. I've grown up doing it. Look out there," she said, waving her hand toward the stretch of blue-green water and the lush green. "This is another world and I can forget the office."

"There are all sorts of ways to forget the office," he said in a husky voice, moving closer.

"Careful, you're coming on again," she said, smiling at him.

"Nothing wrong with that," he said, smiling in return, a devastating, knee-melting smile that made her draw her breath. Creases bracketed his mouth and, with an effort, she tried to concentrate on the boat cutting smoothly through the water. "What else have you been doing, besides sailing? I don't know much about you," he said, leaning his hip against the bulkhead and giving her his undivided attention. It made her heart race.

"I went to Rice, returned home to go to work for Granddad. I bought my own home and I sail on weekends. A simple life. That's about it."

"No special man in your life?"

"No, there isn't," she said, turning to look into his dark eyes, wondering about the women in his life. His mouth was wide, his lower lip full, sensual. What would it be like to kiss him? She struggled to get her thoughts elsewhere.

"Was there an important man?" Nick repeated.

She shook her head again. "Not really. No, there never has been anyone."

"Ah, you're particular."

She smiled. "Or busy."

"The ice princess," he said softly, his dark gaze filled with speculation. "With your heart sealed away. Who will melt your heart of ice and turn you into a warm, passionate woman?"

She laughed. "Are you trying to offer yourself for that role? If so, save your breath."

"I know better than to do that," he replied lightly. "Besides, whoever melts the ice princess then has a responsibility."

"So, Nick Ransome, you have some old-fashioned ideas lurking."

"I keep them locked away rather well," he replied.

"I imagine you do. What about you? I don't know much about you, either."

"My life is an open book. I like closing a deal that I've worked hard to get, making money, flying, sailing, swimming, passionate women, fast horses and faster cars, long, wet kisses, making love in the moonlight and touching. Pretty predictable, I'd say."

"Right, just the guy next door," she remarked facetiously, but her pulse quickened at his answers and the thoughts his remarks conjured up. If only business didn't stand between them, she thought and then realized the dangerous direction of following what-if thoughts.

"What big goals do you have?" he asked. "To be CEO of Holcomb Drilling? To destroy Ransome Energy? To fight with me and win?"

She laughed. "I think you're answering your own questions. Except I don't have ambitions to be a CEO. As for ruining Ransome Energy," she said, looking at him, "that's a tempting one. Especially when you're out to smash us. Now if we can settle our differences peacefully, I'll be quite happy. Otherwise—" She broke off and gazed out at the water, watching waves come up to meet them.

"But if we don't, you're threatening me, aren't you?"

Meeting Nick's gaze squarely, she felt the contest of wills. "We're like two sharks circling each other, part of the time swimming together, part of the time eyeing each other as dinner."

He leaned closer. "You would be the tastiest morsel I ever sunk my teeth into," he drawled in a low, husky voice.

"Careful, Nick, I might bite back," she said seductively, unable to resist dallying with him in return.

"This weekend gets to be a better idea by the second," he said, leaning closer.

She placed her hand against his chest. "You stay right where you are."

He grinned with a disarming flash of white teeth. "I'll check over the place and be back shortly," he said, leaving her at the wheel. She was surprised he trusted her because he didn't know whether she could handle his yacht. Yet in the calm sea, there would be few problems and he was probably counting on that.

Soon he returned, making her heart race as he walked up to her. "I'll take the wheel now," he said, his hands brushing hers lightly. She tingled, aware of the warmth of him as he stood close beside her. "I have a favorite cove," he continued. "It's sheltered, has a beach and we can swim."

"Sounds marvelous," she said, barely knowing how she responded as she watched him.

"See," he said waving his hand and she watched as they followed the shoreline in a sweeping curve.

"It's beautiful," she said when she saw his destination, animosity momentarily forgotten as she turned her attention to the breathtaking view of blue water, white sand and tall, swaying palms. "Your cove is paradise," she said quietly, wishing she were with a companion to share the beauty of the place and make it a weekend of warm memories instead of a chess match with high stakes.

"This is a special escape. I've been sailing here for several years."

"I'm surprised there isn't anyone else here."

"That's part of the charm. Most of the time, this inlet is secluded. And in a few minutes, we can drop anchor," he said, taking the wheel from her and brushing his hands over hers. "I'll give you a tour of my boat and then we can swim," he said.

A few minutes later, he took her arm to go down the companionway to show her the cherrywood and stainless steel galley that opened into the saloon. The galley held a refrigerator, a freezer, a four-burner stove, a built-in table and bench.

"Hopefully, everything we need or want."

"That's your life, isn't it, Nick," she declared. "Everything you need or want at your fingertips. You have to get your way."

He turned his attention to her and arched an eyebrow. He placed his hand on her shoulder. "I suspect in a few areas, we're too much alike. So far, you seem accustomed to getting your way and determined to continue to do so."

"So I guess we're locked in a contest of wills."

"This should be the most delicious, hottest challenge I've ever faced."

"Don't make me a challenge," she cautioned. Aware of his smoldering gaze on her, she moved around the galley, lightly touching the gleaming cherrywood cabinets. "This is a beautiful yacht."

"I like beautiful things, particularly beautiful women," he said in a low voice.

"Well, now that doesn't surprise me one degree." She turned to study him, sensing the sparks flying between them. "I hope this weekend thing was a good idea," she said quietly, her pulse quickening as he stepped closer. When he brushed a tendril of hair away from her face, his fingers skimmed her cheek lightly.

"This weekend is going to be sweet. The wise choice is always to get to know each other and to garner a clear understanding of what your opponent wants."

"We don't have to be opponents, Nick."

"No, we don't," he replied, his voice thick and husky.

"That was not a come-on. Don't mistake it for one," she stated and wished her voice held more force. "If we can just work it out where you don't hurt Granddad," she said, trying to get back to the purpose of her being on Nick's yacht, "I'll try to see that you get business concessions in return that satisfy you completely."

"You want to satisfy me completely?" he said huskily, sending her temperature soaring. Fire danced in the depths of his eyes, and her pulse pounded. He looked at her as if he were about to kiss her.

"Did you even hear the word *business*? I still feel as if I'm swimming with a shark that is eyeing me for dinner," she stated breathlessly.

"There is nothing like a shark about what I want. 'Satisfy me completely'…that opens visions of possibilities."

"You know what I meant! I'm not talking about in bed," she said bluntly. "I meant absolutely no reference to anything personal."

"Too bad. If you had, I might be more easily persuaded." His hand rested on her shoulder and his thumb lightly rubbed her throat, then paused. "It isn't problems with work that has your pulse racing," he drawled, and her heart thumped. Nick saw too much, understood too clearly, guessed too accurately about her. She was held immobile by his hungry, steadfast gaze. That first searing attraction when they met was escalating at an alarming rate.

"We both know that we have some chemistry between us— it doesn't mean a thing," she said.

"I beg to differ," he said softly. "From the moment you ran in front of my car and stopped me, the attraction has been undeniable. My curiosity's stirred. I want to discover the depth of this fire that's between us."

"There is nothing between us except a disagreement we're trying to solve," she argued breathlessly.

"You know better than that," he responded with a wicked arch of one dark eyebrow. "Right now, your pulse races and so does mine."

"I think I'll go on instinct here. Beware the circling shark."

"You're the one who wanted to get close," he reminded her.

"Not quite as close as you have in mind. You're going way too fast. Slow down, Nick. This time two nights ago, we were barely speaking."

She was hot—her heart thudding, her breathing ragged—but she knew she had to get control of herself as well as cool him down. She couldn't stop her body from responding to him, but she should maintain distance between them. A degree of aloofness was becoming increasingly more vital to her well-being. She didn't want to end up two days from now with her heart lost to Nick Ransome. He was everything she didn't want in her life. Business rival. Ambitious, ruthless and into risks. She knew he had been in Special Forces, knew he had a reputation for doing as many wild things as his mountain-climbing brother, who had recently died in an accident.

With effort, she turned away. "Let's finish this tour or the sun will set before we can swim. I like to see what I'm swimming in." When he didn't answer and silence stretched, she was compelled to glance back at him.

As soon as she turned, she found him watching her intently, that smoldering anger back in his expression. Comparing him to a shark was apt—he looked like a predator, a danger to her heart. She had to put distance between them. She didn't trust his motives and his smooth talk. Seduction? The thought shook her, but she reminded herself that if she let him seduce her, she would probably regret it forever because her emotions would be entangled in the act while she was certain his would not.

"Are we going to continue the tour?"

"Sure," he said and led the way below to his forward stateroom. In his stateroom, she stepped away from him while she gazed at the king-size berth, navy and white decor and mirrors on the bulkhead. Too clearly, she could imagine him sprawled out in that bed. The image of his broad, bare chest, lean length, hard muscles, flashed hotly, making her grit her teeth.

Drawing a deep breath, she turned to see two large hanging lockers, plush chairs and a desk.

"As you already know, your stateroom is luxurious and beautiful," she said, glancing at him.

He stood with one shoulder braced against a bulkhead while he watched her. He shrugged lightly. "I don't spend a lot of time in here. C'mon. I'll show you the rest."

She drew a quick breath. The yacht that had appeared so large and accommodating was shrinking with each passing hour. She suspected she and Nick would be together nearly every waking minute and the thought of spending the entire weekend near each other fueled her burning desire.

More aware of Nick than her surroundings, she followed him while he showed her the salon where sunlight streamed in through portholes. He had a game room with a pool table and a plasma television.

When they finished the tour, she returned to her cabin to change to her swimsuit, a black two-piece cut inches below her waist, high over each thigh. It was no more revealing than what many other women wore, but now she longed for a one piece that covered as much of her as possible. The expanses of bare flesh she was presenting would be a come on to Nick.

Why had this weekend seemed such a good idea when she had been alone at home? At that time, she hadn't factored in the scalding response she had to Nick, a reaction that heightened steadily.

"He's just another man and one you don't like very much anyway," she whispered to herself, yet she knew that wasn't true. But he wasn't just another man, and while he angered her, he also appealed to her.

Plaiting her hair into one thick braid, she studied herself in a mirror, turning first one way and then another, knowing she was locked in a contest of wills with him. The outcome of their battle would probably be determined this weekend, no matter what transpired between their lawyers. This was one struggle she intended to win, and the unwanted steamy attraction between her and Nick wasn't going to get in her way or defeat her.

He was a sexy male with a strong liking for women, so he was approachable. She intended to win him over without selling her soul—or her body—to do it.

"You're playing with dynamite," she whispered to herself.

She could resist him because their families had feuded for generations. Her granddad despised Nick, his brother, his father and his grandfather when he had been alive. With that history, she could withstand Nick Ransome's charm. She just hoped he couldn't resist cooperating with her.

She wondered what the evening would bring as she went to

join him, feeling as if she were diving into water that held a shark.

Her conscience told her that Nick would never resort to a shark's tactics. He would never attack and devour. There was never need to. Nick's appeal was the most dangerous kind of all to resist—pure seduction.

Three

As Julia emerged onto the deck, Nick's dark gaze drifted over her like a caress, a slow perusal that sent tingles dancing in its wake. His approval was obvious.

At the same time, she was mesmerized, unable to keep from returning his study, letting her gaze lower across his bare, muscled chest with a mat of brown curly hair. Sunlight splashed over his tanned body, with golden highlights on the swell of hard muscles. His broad chest tapered to a tiny waist and slim hips and a black strip of swimsuit that bulged with his masculinity. His long, muscular legs were covered lightly in short brown hairs. She imagined what it would feel like to be in his arms, pressed against his strong, warm length.

"You're beautiful, Julia," he said quietly. "Definitely an unfair advantage in this battle between us." Moving closer, he reached out to tug lightly on her braid and his knuckles brushed her bare shoulder.

"We're not in a battle today," she said.

"Liar," he accused lightly. "You're taking unfair advantage here."

She stepped closer, looking up at him, only inches of space between them. "No more unfair advantage than you do when you flirt," she said in a sultry voice.

Desire smoldered in his dark eyes. He dropped his towel before placing his hands on her waist. "I have that effect on you?" he asked.

"You know you do. Don't act surprised," she chided, more aware of his hands on her than of what she was saying.

"You're keeping a barrier between us. I want to scale that wall you've surrounded yourself with. I want to get to know you."

"Nick," she cautioned. "We have to step back and get a lid on the sex and emotion."

"Let go a little and let's see where they take us," he coaxed. He reached out to let his fingers slowly trace her jawline. "Let's start with a swim."

She was tempted to tell him to turn the yacht around and head back. She didn't want a weekend with him coming on to her and turning her into breathless mush, a melting, responsive female who boosted his ego and gave him the upper hand in their dealings. She knew enough about him to know there was a steady stream of women in his life. She didn't want to fall into his arms and his bed, and then be tossed aside like an old shoe. Only an old shoe didn't feel anything. She had always avoided heartbreak, and she could imagine the casualties in Nick's background.

He lowered the ladder over the side and stepped back. "You can go into the water this way," he said, motioning with a wave of his hand.

"Do you climb down that?"

"I dive."

"Then I will, too," she said. He laughed, touching her cheek lightly with his forefinger.

"Ever competitive. Let's go." He stepped to the side, going over in a smooth dive, his muscles flexing. Her mouth went dry as she looked at his long, powerful body in prime physical condition.

Trying to stop her flood of thoughts about him, she followed him, feeling refreshingly cool water closing over her. She came up to find him swimming away from her, parallel to the beach, and she followed, catching up with him and swimming beside him. What compelled her to compete with him on every level? She wanted to best him in every way, wring what she wanted out of him, make him as breathless when they flirted as he made her. She suspected on the last, she did. Only she knew his flirting might have a deeper effect on her. She was certain that she couldn't be as casual about sex as he could be.

He turned to swim back to her. "Want to snorkel or just swim?"

"Snorkel," she replied.

Nick splashed out of the water, clambering back on board to return in minutes with breathing equipment for both of them.

As she swam under the surface, she looked with wonder at the world of water she had entered. Brightly colored fish, in deep blues and bright yellows swam gracefully near. She clutched Nick's arm to look at one with brilliant orange-and-black stripes. Then she forgot the water and the dazzling array of fish as her hand closed on his arm. He was sleek and warm and muscular. She released him immediately, but he caught her arm and pulled her close again.

While her heart raced, she looked into his eyes. They couldn't talk and even submerged in cool water, she was hot, burning with desire that was a constant torment.

She pushed away from him and went to the surface. Nick splashed up beside her. Breathless, she stared at him. "It's beautiful down there," she gasped.

"It's beautiful up here," he said solemnly.

She placed her finger over his lips, conscious of a current that tingled through her hand. She went under again, gliding away from him. They swam close together, looking at tropical, salt-water fish that were a myriad of bright colors.

When they put away their snorkeling equipment, Nick swam away from her, heading out toward the open water where waves were choppier. She wondered how well he knew the water they were in. Even though he hadn't said anything, she felt as if he were daring her to follow him.

Wisdom told her to stay in the cove where they had been swimming and where the water was more calm, but her competitiveness made her want to keep up with him.

She swam out beside him and treaded water, thankful there wasn't a stronger chop and wondering how deep the water was. The yacht and shoreline appeared to be a long way back.

"You're a damn good swimmer," he said, moving beside her. "And either not scared of this or determined to keep up with me."

"I figured you hoped to drown me," she said, and he laughed while they bobbed in the water.

"Not at all. You're far too interesting alive. Let's race back."

"You know you'll win. You want to win every time, don't you?"

"No more than you do. I'll give you a head start."

She was getting tired of treading water and the open water was choppier than it had looked when they were on the boat. She turned to swim back slowly, watching him slice through the water spreading the distance between them. She wondered why he swam out so far, but then decided he liked challenges. Did he view her as a challenge? she wondered. Probably not.

She swam to him as he waited.

"Have you worked up an appetite for dinner yet?" he asked.

She was standing flat-footed in water that came to her shoulders, and he stood only a few feet away. Water droplets sparkled on his bare shoulders and his curly brown hair was plastered to his head, making him appear sleek and dangerous. Drops of water sparkled on his thick eyelashes and were sprinkled over his skin.

"Now that you mention it, yes. By the time we dress and cook dinner, definitely," she answered, wondering if she was going to have this heart-pounding reaction to him the entire weekend—or longer.

"Let's head for my boat," he said, turning to swim away. When they climbed back on board, he said he would get dinner.

In minutes, their suits were dry, and she pulled on her low-cut, hip-hugging cutoffs and a T-shirt, turning to find him watching her.

"I was hoping you'd eat like you were," he said.

"No way. You can."

"That's definitely not the same." He vanished inside and returned shortly in a T-shirt and cutoffs and his deck shoes. As the orange sun slanted low in the west sending a golden streak of fire across the surface of the blue water, Nick put steaks on to grill and served her a glass of red wine.

Tempting smells made her mouth water and the quiet was relaxing, wrapping around them. On the deck overlooking the water, four chairs with tables between two of them were in a small circle. She sat on a chair and he sat facing her and raised his glass. "Here's to mutual satisfaction in our endeavor."

"I'll drink to that," she said, raising her drink in a toast and taking only a small sip.

"Tell me about your life, Julia," he said, studying her with that dark-eyed intensity that gave her goose bumps. He set his glass on a table. "What do you want in the future?"

"That's an easy question. I want to marry and have a family, although I'm only twenty-eight, so I'm not in a rush."

"I'm thirty-two, and not only in no rush, my freedom is essential," he replied firmly. "No marriage for me."

"That sounds final and bitter," she said, wondering why he was so sour on marriage. "I know you like women."

"I just want my freedom. I come from a family of nonmarrying people except for my brother, who has had one disastrous union and is married again. My parent's marriage was even more of a calamity than my brother's. I say no thanks to the ball and chain."

"You view someone you love as a 'ball and chain,'" she repeated with amusement. "You may have a lonely life," she predicted, yet she knew the handsome man she faced would never be lonely. "I want a family because I have almost none. My only living relatives are my granddad and my granddad's sister. I want a big family. You have a brother and sister—aren't you close to them?"

He shrugged one muscled shoulder. "I suppose, but we go for periods of time without seeing each other. We keep in touch."

"I'm sorry about the brother you lost—the one that died in the mountain climbing accident."

"Yeah. We all miss Jeff. Well, good luck with getting married and having kids. With your looks, there'll be no problem about marrying."

"Thank you, I think."

"You're beautiful, but your brain may scare off some guys."

"Not the right one," she answered with amusement. "He'll be smarter than I am, I imagine."

"I'd take bets on that," he said, and she smiled. He touched her cheek, and she felt a frisson of excitement from the slight contact. "That smile should get you everything in life you want."

She flashed him another broad smile. "Do you think so? Will it get what I want from you?"

"I walked right into that one," he remarked, leaning closer. He was only inches from her. "It probably will," he said in a husky voice as he looked at her mouth. She wanted to kiss him, even though she knew she should keep her distance.

"So what do you want, Nick? No family. Freedom to do what?" she asked too breathlessly, but hoping to get back to more impersonal topics.

"To build an oil empire," he said immediately. "To have the toys and homes I want. I want success."

"We measure success differently, Nick. To you, it's money and acquisitions and a career. I measure success in love and family and relationships and people. We're worlds apart."

He gave her a mocking smile and traced his forefinger back and forth on her forearm, distracting her from what he was saying.

"You'd like to accomplish what you set out to achieve or you wouldn't be with me right now," he observed. "You're out here because you intend to fight for your company and your grandfather. We're the same."

"No, we're not," she argued quietly. "If it weren't for Granddad, I wouldn't be here. I can give up the company. I'd just move on. It's for him. We're not remotely the same, Nick. What you value in life is not what I hold dear."

Nick picked up her hand and spread her fingers against his, examining her hand and running his fingers lightly over her knuckles. She knew she should move her hand away, but she couldn't.

"I like challenges and winning. That's not so bad," he said, watching her.

"Whether it's bad or good depends on how you go about acquiring what you want."

"I'm sure to you and your family, it's bad. I'd guess you view me as Mr. Greed," he said. When his gaze ran the length of her, she tingled from head to toe.

"Business aside, we might do all right," he speculated, looking at her mouth and then letting his gaze slide slowly to her legs.

"Oh, sure," she said facetiously, knowing he knew as well as she did the impossibility of what he suggested. "As if either one of us could forget that I'm a Holcomb and you're a Ransome. The animosity between our families goes back too many generations for that to happen. Plus, I see marriage in my future. I don't take relationships lightly. I'm sure you're the opposite."

"You and I could change the dynamics between our families and end the fuss."

"Like you're suddenly going to love Granddad, and I'll be ever so happy with your family. I wouldn't count on it," she said.

"I suppose you're right. I'll check on the steaks." He stood and she watched him cross the deck. On his boat, he had a rolling gait and kept his balance well, moving around with ease. Another big plume of smoke rose from the grill and the smells made her mouth water. She surmised the weekend would be a bust. She couldn't imagine Nick changing his views about her family or their company any more than she intended to change her opinions of him or his family. They had agreed to not discuss business for the first twenty-four hours, yet so far, they had hassled over everything they did, including something as simple as swimming. How could she hope for a business compromise or an agreement from him?

She scanned his bare legs. One thing was certain—he was too sexy to easily resist.

Julia went to offer her help. When he turned her down, she moved to the rail to sip her wine and lookout at the beach and the water, thinking that all the beauty of their surroundings was being wasted on two people who were at cross-purposes.

"Enjoying the view?" he said softly behind her.

She turned to face him, leaning back with her elbows on the rail. "Yes. It's enchanting here."

"I like charming places and gorgeous women." He moved closer and put his hands on the rail, hemming her in.

"Nick—"

"Scared of me?"

"No, I'm not. But we're very different and I don't want to get closely involved with you."

"Do you tell this to all the guys?"

"No," she replied. "I don't go out with ones where we're 'very different.' This weekend with you is unique," she said, aware of his proximity, the breeze catching locks of his curly hair and blowing them slightly. She looked at his brown hair framing his face and could imagine her fingers tangled in its thick softness. What was it about him that constantly drew her?

"This weekend is singular," he agreed in a low voice, "and I still insist that we can be friends." His hands slid from the rail to her waist and she inhaled deeply while her heart skipped a beat.

"Careful, Nick," she warned, trying to ignore her racing pulse. "I imagine you rarely play by the rules."

"*Au contraire!* I certainly do follow rules. Pay my taxes, help little old ladies across the street, take my dad fishing," he said while his gaze roamed over her features.

"What an upstanding, law-abiding citizen—most of the time. But then there are the moments when you are over the speed limit, when you turn on your sexy charm and when you devour your competitors," she declared.

His hands rested lightly on her waist and his thumbs moved languidly back and forth on her ribs. His touch created havoc with her concentration.

He laughed. "Sexy charm? Guilty as charged, I hope! I'm not going to stop coming on to a gorgeous blonde. Not in this lifetime. It's far too interesting, and who knows where it might lead? Now here's where I hope it leads. I hope said blonde has to succumb to the flirting, and I do believe there is a bit of flirting in return from this beautiful blonde."

Amused, she smiled at him. "It will lead nowhere. Is dinner burning?"

"Probably," he said, studying her and not moving.

Her pulse drummed because he stood too close and was looking at her too intently. She placed her hand against his chest, feeling the warmth of him beneath the cotton T-shirt. "Dinner, Nick," she reminded him. "I don't want charred steak."

"If I got something else instead, I wouldn't care," he said in a husky voice.

"If the something else is a hamburger or some such, I'd just as soon have my steak," she said, trying to keep the moment light. She stepped away at the same time he turned and strode back to the grill.

Watching his sure-footed stride, she drifted along behind him, taking in his cutoffs, his trim backside. She inhaled while desire coiled like a dangerous flame low inside her.

Trying to focus on something besides Nick, she saw the steaks were ready and she helped him get everything on a table. As they ate, a breeze blew over them and the sun was a mere orange slice on the horizon.

She bit into the thick, juicy steak and wished she and Nick had known each other under other circumstances. But such was not the case, and nothing could take away the past or change how she felt about him.

"I'll admit, this has been a wonderful day, Nick."

"Good. See, it's possible to get along."

"Yes—as long as not one word is said about business," she

added with amusement. "Tell me about yourself. Where did you go to school and where were you stationed with Special Forces?"

"I went to Texas University. In the military, I was stationed several places, but spent most of my time in North Carolina."

"Is your dad active in Ransome Energy now?"

"No. Dad retired to his ranch the minute I could take charge. He and my brother run the family place—mostly my brother Matt. Dad just enjoys himself. His health hasn't been so great. I have the feeling that you already know all that about me and my family."

"Only the most general information. You said your father divorced. Do you see your mother often?"

A shuttered look crossed Nick's features and he glanced away. "I haven't seen her since I was very small and she walked out on us. She made it absolutely clear that she didn't want to see any of us."

"Sorry," Julia replied. "I can't imagine a mother doing that," she added, wondering how much that event contributed to his grim outlook on marriage. She tilted her head. "I saw her once."

His dark eyebrow arched quizzically, but the flash of surprise was gone instantly. "How would you even know her?"

"Granddad. I was a teen traveling with Granddad and we were at the airport when Granddad said hello to her and they talked briefly. At the time, I thought she was incredibly beautiful."

He merely shrugged.

"Granddad said she was hurt by the breakup."

"Your grandfather doesn't know at all. She was far from hurt."

"None of you have ever had any contact with her since that time?"

"No. Julia, she left us—not the other way around," he stated flatly with a harsh note in his voice and she suspected he had been badly hurt at the time.

"You were little children. Maybe your father didn't tell you the whole story."

"He might not have told us the whole story, but he told us enough. Forget her. She's no part of our lives and never will be."

"She was a big part at one time."

His annoyance heightened and his dark eyes flashed. "I don't care to even think about her. Subject closed."

"Sorry, Nick. I didn't intend to intrude."

He shrugged and placed his hand on her shoulder, massaging it lightly. "And I came on too strong, but she's no part of our lives."

"You're strong-willed. My guess is that you've surrounded yourself with people who do what you want constantly and with women who are gaga and likewise try to please you. You're not accustomed to dealing with someone who doesn't follow your express wishes."

"And you're going to oppose me every way you can," he said, a twinkle appearing in his eyes.

"I think it just comes naturally," she replied, amused in turn. "We're opposites, Nick. There's no common ground."

"There a delicious common ground that is the chemistry boiling between us. Sparks dance and you can't deny that you feel them. Every time I get your pulse, it's racing. Is that a permanent condition? Or the result of us?"

Her pulse quickened at his words, but she didn't want to admit the truth to him.

"I don't know what you plan for Ransome Energy. What direction do you plan to take it?"

"You're running, Julia. Scared to face the truth about what you feel right now? Or scared to admit it? You're changing the subject."

"It's time we changed it. Answer my question, please."

He stared at her a moment while her pulse drummed because every word he said was true. "I want a worldwide company that will grow," he finally said.

They talked and ate little of their dinners. Afterwards, she helped him clean up.

"It's been more than an hour since we ate," he said finally. "Let's go in for a quick dip. We have a full moon coming up over the horizon and the water is cool."

She looked at the dark water and shivered slightly. She didn't like to swim in water that wasn't clear and she didn't like to swim at night, which frightened her as much as opaque, muddy water, but she didn't want to admit her vulnerability to a man whom she suspected feared very few things.

"Talked me into it," she said standing, trying to keep in mind how swimming had been earlier with golden sunlight streaming through the crystal depths. "I will race you into the water," she said, peeling her shirt off and tossing it aside before she glanced at him. Her hands were on her shorts as she paused.

He watched her without moving. Desire burned hotly in his brown eyes.

"There are other things we could do," he said in a husky voice and she tingled. His hungry gaze held her and the smoldering attraction blazed, threatening the control she was trying to maintain.

"Julia," he said softly, taking a step toward her.

Her mouth went dry and desire shook her, but common sense held sway. She waved her hand at him, motioning him to stop. "I vote for the race and this time I have a chance of winning," she said, unfastening her shorts with shaking fingers, too aware of his scalding gaze. She dropped the shorts as fast as possible, stepped out of them, kicked off the deck shoes and rushed to jump overboard. She didn't want to think about how Nick was looking at her, about peeling off her outer layer of clothes right in front of him, or about jumping into black Gulf waters that held a myriad of creatures.

Cool water closed over her and then she pushed up and burst to the surface. Shaking her head and slicking back her hair, she treaded water, fighting a sense of panic about the inky water surrounding her. Then she glanced back at the yacht and her fears evaporated.

Backlit by lamps on the boat, Nick stood poised at the side. The impact of the view was broad shoulders, long legs, a man who was strong and desirable. The last few minutes had made her blood run hot with longing. She wished she knew him under other circumstances.

Nick sliced into the water and came up close beside her. "I'll race you to the beach. It'll give us a workout."

"You're on," she replied, wondering on how many levels she would compete with him during the weekend.

"I'll give you a head start. You go," he said.

"I'll go when you do. You can beat me, but I don't want a head start."

He laughed and began swimming toward the beach. She tried to keep up with him, but he soon widened the distance between them. She swam enough at home that she was fast and in good physical shape, but his powerful muscles told her the same was true of Nick. His arms sliced through the water and he won easily, walking up on the sandy beach and sitting down.

She followed, knowing he was watching her walk toward him. Silvery moonlight splashed over him, highlighting powerful muscles, revealing his long, bare body. The scrap of swimsuit looked like a dark shadow. Everything they did stirred her desire, making her more and more conscious of him. This moment was one more scalding temptation.

She sat beside him to look at the water with a slash of a brilliant moonlight streaming across it. Even so, the dark water sent a shiver down her spine. "You win again, if you're keeping score."

"No. I don't keep score in little things. It's the big things that matter."

"Why do I doubt that?" she asked, leaning back on her hands and still looking at the water, amazed she had been able to swim in it and, for a few minutes, lose her apprehension.

"You were right behind me."

"Trailing you quite a bit," she remarked. "Earlier today, I thought maybe there was hope for us to reach a state where we're on friendly footing. Since sailing with you this afternoon, it's beginning to look hopeless. We compete in everything."

"No, we don't. There are some things we do great together," he said.

"Like what—eat steaks and drink wine?" she said.

"There's this," he said, drawing his fingers in a feathery

caress along her ear and throat and down her arm. Inhaling deeply, she turned her head to look at him and her heartbeat raced.

He leaned closer and placed his hand on her throat. "You and I have the same response to each other. Admit it," he demanded softly.

Excitement built inside her as she was locked in his stare. "Mine is unwanted," she whispered. "We're poles apart in too many ways and in one of the most important aspects of all." She pulled away from his touch even though desire flamed through her veins. She couldn't keep from looking at his mouth. Her breath caught, and with an effort she tore her gaze away.

"Business is nothing next to this," he said and his words cut through the haze of wanting him, the temptation to lean closer and kiss him.

"I think there is never a moment when victory is nothing to you," she whispered, unable to draw a deep breath, physically responding to him, yet mentally fighting herself.

"Dammit, there are times when I forget ambition," he argued in a low voice as he turned to face her and scooted close. He slid his hand behind her head. His fingers were warm on her nape. He was too close, his mouth only inches away. They were both almost naked—warm, bare bodies with his knee touching her, his hand caressing her. He wanted her and the hungry longing in his eyes made his desire plain to see.

She ached to kiss him. He was only inches from her. What would a kiss hurt? He searched her gaze and pulled lightly on the back of her head.

Closing her eyes, she twisted away and stood. "Dark water scares me," she said softly, "but I think I'm a lot safer out there than here."

"*Safe?* I'd never hurt you," he said, standing and placing his hand on her waist.

"You can break my heart and you know it," she replied, her voice as raspy and breathless as his.

"You're a beautiful, desirable woman. I know men have been

in your life before, so you're not going to get a broken heart if we kiss a few times this weekend," he persisted.

His arm slid around her waist. "I don't have that big an effect on you, do I?" he asked in a teasing voice, but he watched her closely.

She shook her head. "No, you don't. I wouldn't tell you if you did and you know it."

She placed her hand against his bare chest to stop him from drawing her into his embrace, but the moment she touched his rock-hard muscles and felt his heart pounding, she wanted him more than ever.

"No!" she whispered and stepped back, turning to dash into the water to cool her scorching body. She splashed away, swimming toward the boat, for the first time that she could remember, she forgot her fear of opaque water.

Soon he swam beside her. He brushed against her. "Want to get back on board?"

"Yes," she replied.

He swam ahead, scrambled up the ladder and turned to lean down when she climbed up. He lifted her easily to the deck and watched her, keeping his hands on her waist. She caught his wrists and removed his hands.

"Nick," she said quietly.

"I'm curious. I want to know what it's like to kiss you. I want to see how much response I can evoke from you. I want you in my arms where I can feel your softness," he said, his voice dropping back to that husky tone that made her toes curl while his words drew pictures in her mind and made her want him to do just what he said.

"Instead, I'm going to get dressed," she replied with that same breathlessness that he could constantly stir. She hurried away to her cabin.

As she dressed in fresh cutoffs and a T-shirt, she wished she could develop an immunity to him. She couldn't put his sexy drawl or what he said to her out of mind, hearing it over and over. He was trying to seduce her. He had said "a few kisses," but she knew once she started, it would never stop at kisses. The attraction between them was too hot and too strong. Why did it have to be Nick Ransome who turned her into a quivering, melting woman with an insatiable craving for what he offered?

She reminded herself of all the reasons to resist. "He's a playboy," she said to herself. "A man driven by ambition and a compulsion to win and conquer challenges and women." She dried her hair, staring at her reflection, but seeing Nick and his fit, powerful body. "He's too desirable, too seductive, too smart. He goes after what he wants and right now what he wants—" she paused and leaned closer to the mirror, looking herself in the eye "—is me."

"He wants me and he's turning all his sexy charm on to get his way. And it's working too darn well." Thinking about him, she tingled. She wanted to join him on deck. She was playing with fire and he had her wanting him passionately. She should go to bed, alone, and stay away from him for the rest of the night. She should, but she couldn't. The man was too exciting, and maybe he had some of the same need and longing.

"Oh, right!" she said aloud. "How many women have thought that one!"

She intended to soften him up with this weekend together, get him more willing to compromise on a deal. Soften Nick? Ridiculous! The man was hard inside and out! His body was as hard as his feelings for business rivals.

All the time she argued with herself, Julia continued getting ready to join him again.

Before she left her cabin, she paused to look at herself and give herself one last admonition. "Beware of charm," she said. "Resist him no matter how sexy and hot he is, in spite of how much you want him." Trying to rein in her eagerness, she headed above to join him.

Since part of her couldn't wait to see him, she wondered if she could resist him.

Four

She found him sitting on deck. He had cut the lights except the ones needed for safety, but moonlight illuminated the night, giving the boat a cozy, dreamlike ambience. The moment she appeared, Nick came to his feet.

He wore only cutoffs and his muscles were highlighted by the moonlight. At the sight of him, Julia's mouth went dry. She hoped he couldn't hear her pounding heartbeat.

When he reached out to lift locks of her hair, she thrilled at the faint tugs on her scalp. "Your hair is soft," he whispered, letting it slide through his fingers. "Come sit with me," he said, taking her arm to walk a few feet to deck chairs.

A barrel table with a cleared surface was between two chairs. Nick took a cushion from a chair and placed it on the top of the table and sat on it to face her, putting him close to her.

"What are you doing?" she asked in amusement. "The chair looks more comfortable."

"But this is more interesting. It puts me nearer to you, and I can touch you a little," he said, drawing his forefinger over the back of her hand that rested on the arm of her chair.

"You never stop!" she exclaimed, smiling at him.

"I'm fascinated."

"Oh, please. You're after my family's company."

"When I sat down here, there was not one thought in my mind about business," he drawled in a velvety tone. "You're beautiful, sexy and I want to sit close and touch a little and maybe I'll get to kiss you."

His voice dropped a notch. "Sooner or later, Julia, we're going to discover how much fire there really is between us."

She hoped he didn't guess how excited she was. "Sit in your chair, Nick, and look at the stars."

"You want me to keep my distance?" Before she could reply, he slipped his hand behind her head to caress her nape in feathery touches that fanned flames higher in her. "I don't think so," he continued. "When we're together, I know your pulse quickens. I know you breathe faster. I know—"

"You're too observant," she whispered, on the verge of leaning the last few inches and drawing him to her to kiss him. Instead, she removed his hand and wiggled her fingers at him. "You back off. You may make my pulse race, but I know what's good for me."

Smiling at her, he straightened and kept his hands to himself. "You eat right, you exercise, you don't take risks—I don't believe it, Julia. You're at sea alone with me. You swim with me in your scrap of a suit that is a red-hot invitation and branded into my memory."

"When I bought this suit, I didn't know you."

"You knew me when you packed it. I'm not complaining, believe me. It's the best-looking swimsuit I've ever seen."

"You're absolutely incorrigible!"

"Your protests have nothing to do with the way you react to me," he observed dryly. "I can wait. I'm patient." He leaned close again and his warm breath fanned her ear. "We're going to kiss. I'll bet the boat on that one." Before she could tell him to get away, he took her wrist, felt her pulse and gave her a mocking smile. Then he slid into the empty chair.

"I suspect you are far too accustomed to women succumbing to your every whim."

"How I wish!"

"When I look at you, I see a man driven by ambition. Your life is wrapped around your career. That's cold companionship, Nick."

"I want good friends, beautiful women and good times together, but I'll admit I like the wheeling and dealing in business. I told you, I like success."

"I'm sure you *love* success."

He leaned forward and reached out to draw circles on her knee. "Today you said you didn't want to be CEO of Holcomb, so in the big picture, what do you want?" he asked, watching her closely.

"That's an easy question. I want people in my life I can love. I hope I have children. If it works out, I want a man who loves me above all else. I want him to be the most important person in my life and I want to be the most essential person in his life. And I want *us*, together, to be foremost always."

"So someone can come before your love for Rufus."

"That's different and you know it. You'll always love your family, won't you?"

"Oh, sure."

"So why do I suspect that the deepest love of your life is yourself?" she asked softly.

"Ouch! That hurt! Damn, do I act that egotistical and self-centered?" he asked, narrowing his eyes.

"No, in fairness, you don't, but you don't care to have the love of one particular woman forever—"

"Drop the *forever*," he said, watching her. "I'd like to have the love of one particular woman," he added huskily.

More tingles spiraled in Julia because she knew he directed the statement at her. She laughed softly, trying to defuse the impact of his words. "You flirt shamelessly!"

"Shamelessly is more exciting. C'mon and enjoy yourself.

You like being here with me. We're clicking. I don't think you know how to enjoy life."

"And you're going to show me?" she asked, shaking her head.

"Anytime and anyway you let me," he drawled in that velvety tone again. She was tempted to give in and just enjoy him and the weekend without any thought for tomorrow.

He leaned closer, reached out and touched her throat lightly. "Be friends with me, Julia."

She gazed into his dark eyes and wondered if she would feel the same with a tiger purring beside her—strong, beautiful, inviting to pet, but with claws hidden and power leashed. Nick was the same. How far could she trust him? How involved should she get and how much would she regret it later?

The last question brought reality crashing back. She pulled her gaze away from him. When she did, he stood.

"Can I get you something to drink? Either hot or cold?"

"Just some iced tea," she replied. He nodded and left her alone. She let out her breath, feeling her heartbeat slow and her temperature drop to normal. He knew she reacted to him, but did he have a clue about how strongly she responded? She hoped not. She would bet money that he kept his word and sooner or later, they would kiss. He had come close to goading her into it tonight. Actually, closer than before. If he were anyone else—

She stopped that train of thought and looked around. The night was beautiful, with a moonbeam reflecting on the dark surface of the water. Overhead millions of stars twinkled, a sight impossible to view in town. Everything was perfect except the unbridgeable chasm between them. It went beyond business competition—their personalities clashed. His dreams and goals were what she wanted to avoid in any male she got deeply involved with. Her dreams and aspirations probably made him want to run. Actually, she suspected he ignored her views of commitment, considering them insignificant. He had probably had relationships with women before who had wanted exactly what she herself did—marriage, family, abiding love. Nick wanted none of them, and he easily dismissed her goals and dreams.

She needed to remember their differences all the time because on a purely physical level, their desire was mutual, compelling.

Interrupting her thoughts, he returned with their drinks.

When he handed her a glass, his warm fingers brushed hers. He set his tea on the table between them and sat in the chair.

"Thanks," she said.

"Why the fear of dark water?" he asked casually.

She shivered. "I don't even like to talk about it."

"Then don't. I can't keep from wanting to know all about you," he added quietly.

"How can I resist telling you now?" she asked. Before he could answer, she continued, "My fear isn't a secret, just unpleasant to recall. When I was a kid, I fell into some muddy water with a friend. We were on a rickety log over a brown creek. She tumbled into a nest of snakes and was bitten and had to go to the hospital. I wasn't tangled in the snakes, but it terrified me. Since that time, I've never liked opaque water. A childish fear that hangs on."

"If that's the case, you hid it well. If you hadn't told me, I wouldn't have known it. And you should've told me. We can do other things that you'll enjoy more."

"Actually, you took my mind off the water and my fears several times."

"Did I now?" he asked with great innocence, and she laughed.

"You know you did! Anyway, if I don't want to swim, I'll tell you. So now you tell me—what do you fear, Nick?"

"Losing. I don't like to lose," he said. His tone was light, but she knew he gave her a truthful answer.

"We all lose at one time or another," she said. "I suspect you've lost very few times in your life."

"That doesn't make me like it," he replied, and she heard the note of steely determination in his tone. "Most of the time I'm happy with what I'm doing."

"You have a boat and a plane and a ranch. What else do you enjoy, Nick?"

"Bronc riding," he said, surprising her. She figured he would prefer city life and everything connected with it, and very little about the country. "I like racing horses."

"I'm sure you mean winning races."

"Of course. At the ranch, I raise quarter horses and race them. So what do you like?"

"I think you already know. I sail. I work out, and I imagine you do also. I love opera."

"Favorite composer?" he asked, taking her hand and threading his fingers through hers.

"What are you doing?" she asked immediately.

"Just holding your hand. It's as pleasant as looking at the stars and just as harmless. What composer do you prefer?"

"Mozart, definitely," she replied, tingling from his thumb lightly rubbing back and forth over her hand. He disturbed her, kept her physically aware of him every minute, fanned the attraction that grew hotter by the hour.

"Good choice. Verdi is another fine choice. Mozart's *Magic Flute* will be performed at the Santa Fe Opera next week. Want to fly out with me and see it?"

Her immediate inclination was to accept his offer. The prospect of flying to Santa Fe with Nick and attending the opera, spending another weekend with him, dangled like a golden gift. Her eagerness bubbled, but common sense prevailed. The last thing she should do would be fly out of state with him and spend another couple of days in his company. She was enjoying this weekend beyond her wildest expectations. Another weekend, and she would want to be with him all the time.

"Thanks so much for the invitation, but I have to pass. When we part Sunday, we might not be on good terms," she replied while her heart thumped.

"Scaredy-cat," he teased lightly, caressing her cheek. "We're getting along fine now, and we have since the moment you arrived at the yacht club. There's no reason to think that will change. We enjoy each other." His voice lowered. "I get the feeling that you're very careful about what you do."

"Being careful keeps me out of trouble. There's no way that you and I should spend more time together than we will this weekend."

"The invitation stands. If you change your mind, just say so."

"Thank you," she answered politely, wanting to get off the topic of spending more time with him or speculating on how well they could get along. "Tell me about your quarter horses."

"Do you have one degree of interest in horses, or is this a mere tactic to get the conversation back on an impersonal level?"

"Definitely a tactic to get back on the impersonal," she answered bluntly. "Therefore, tell me about your horses. Which one are you running this season?"

"Willow Wind will be running in Ruidoso next and he's good. He's undefeated so far. That's the way I want his races to continue."

"Well, you said you don't like to lose at anything," she said, watching him while he reached down to trace circles on her knee and rev up her pulse.

"No, I don't, and neither do you."

"Compulsive personality, Nick. Have to be the best, don't want to lose, determined to get your way."

"Normal, just like everybody else, impressed with beautiful blondes who are equally resolute."

She laughed. "Not in this lifetime have I ever been as firm about getting what I want as you are!"

"You firm? You're as soft as warm butter," he said quietly. "At least I made you laugh. That's good. You're too serious, Julia."

"It's the circumstances that make me solemn. A lot is on the line."

"Not tonight, it isn't."

"Just stick to horses, Nick," she urged, continuing to try to keep the conversation away from the difficulty between them.

For the next hour, she listened while he talked about his horses. All the time they chatted, he touched her casually. Conversation drifted from horses to their childhoods and then to other topics. All the while, Nick continued to rub his fingers on her hand, or trail them along her arm or through her hair.

Each stroke of his fingers built responding need in her until she was on fire with wanting him. In the darkness, she could see his profile and his long, bare body covered only by his cutoffs. As he talked, she noticed his thick lashes that were dark shadows above his prominent cheekbones. There was a dangerous, predatory air about him, a rugged edge to his handsomeness that hinted at what she suspected was a ruthless streak in him. Brown curls had fallen across his forehead and she was tempted to reach up and push his hair back. What would he do if she touched him? To resist the temptation, she locked her fingers together in her lap.

They talked, skipping from topic to topic, avoiding any reference to the big issue between them.

Nick stood, disappearing into the pilothouse and returning as music played. He took her hand. "Come dance with me."

Laughing, she stood. "In deck shoes?"

"It'll work if you pick up your feet," he said, and she wondered how many times and with how many different women he had danced on his yacht. He pulled her to him and wrapped an arm around her waist, holding her close against his bare chest. Her T-shirt and lacy bra were a thin barrier between them, and contact with him heated her. She moved with him, their legs brushing, her hand held in his.

"So what are your favorite things, Julia?" he asked softly, his warm breath fanning over her. "Every time I try to get to know you, you steer conversation back to horses or me or something impersonal."

"Impersonal is safer, innocuous and forgettable."

"And that's what you want your evening with me to be—innocuous and forgettable? I think not!"

"That's *exactly* what I want this night together to be," she answered, and he shook his head.

"Oh, no," he murmured. "Not when we can have so much

more. I want to satisfy all my curiosity about you," he said, drawing his fingers down her cheek. "What do you like best in daily life?"

He was close to her, inches away, speaking lowly as his gaze drifted over her features. Then he looked into her eyes. His hand slipped to her nape again, brushing her with the same feathery touches that wreaked so much emotional havoc. She looked at his full underlip, his sculpted mouth, and wondered again what it would feel like to kiss him. He had asked her a question, and she struggled to concentrate on what he had said.

"My favorite things are being with my family or my closest friends, bluebonnets, Mozart, skiing, walking in the snow," she replied. "It's your turn to tell me your favorites in life."

"My favorites are making love to a passionate woman, deep kisses, success, meeting a challenge and winning, racing horses."

"And winning at it," she finished for him. "Winning, winning, winning. I think we could have answered for each other." She tilted her head. "Perhaps you couldn't have guessed my answer, but I could have predicted yours."

"Ouch! I'm predictable?"

"Absolutely! When it comes to women and business and what you hold dear, you've made it abundantly clear what you like."

He spun her around and bent over her, dipping deeply so that she tightened her grip on his shoulder. He held her that way, leaning over her as if he were going to kiss her and her heart pounded.

He swung her up and they continued dancing, desire, hot and thrumming, building between them.

"I'll have to work on that one and see if I can't surprise you. Predictable is dull. Like being nice and being good. You've given me another challenge."

"A quite unintentional one, Nick. It's not so bad that we're beginning to know each other and what the other one likes. By now, you know I put family as my top priority. I know you put winning."

"I don't believe I said winning as my number one choice."

She smiled. "You would never consider making love as important as winning a business deal you've fought for. I can well imagine how your mind works on it. There are always beautiful women in your life, so the real challenge is in your work. Don't deny it. I'm certain I'm right."

He gave her a mocking smile. "If women succumb to my charms constantly and easily, why don't you?" he asked huskily.

She inhaled and smiled and hoped she could keep her voice light. "Not every woman you encounter is going to be swept off her feet. There might be one or two of us, Nick, that don't wait breathlessly for your attention."

He laughed. "Damn straight you don't! I can't get to first base with you. Which just makes you all the more interesting. That, plus the chemistry is volatile. And so obvious that even you can't deny it."

"No, but I don't have to yield to it and I have no curiosity about it and no inclination to follow up on it. Chemistry is physical. My emotions and my intellect are still motoring along. Sorry, Nick. Stop making me one of your projects."

He smiled at her. "A luscious, irresistible, impossible challenge—the best of all possible 'projects,' I'd say."

His words heated her. She smiled in return, but the tension between them still dangled in the air.

The music changed to a fast number and in spite of the deck shoes, they danced around each other, moving fast, her pulse throbbing faster as she watched his lithe, muscled body and his sexy movements.

She was aware of his smoldering look following her, his eyes traveling over her, speculation and desire burning in the depths of brown eyes. Fast or slow, the dances were seduction, more kindling on an already searing fire.

Another slow dance began and he enfolded her in his embrace, pressing her against his length and barely moving while he feathered kisses over her ear. She ached with desire. She longed to wrap her arms around his neck and pull his head down to kiss him. Instead, she pushed against his chest and stepped back when he loosened his hold on her.

"I think it's time to sit out a few dances," she said breathlessly and turned away without waiting for his answer as she headed back to a chair and sat down.

Facing her, he sat and rested his elbows on his knees. "Why do I think you really could dance the night away and not sit out any dances?"

She shrugged. "Nonetheless, here we are. No more dancing for now. Back to some impersonal topic."

Leaning closer, he ran his fingers over her knuckles and she inhaled swiftly. "When we get home, go out with me. How about dinner Sunday night?"

"Sorry, Nick. I have a date with Granddad. I told him I'd come by when I get home. I won't let him down."

"So I strike out again with you."

"Something you're completely unaccustomed to having happen in your successful life."

"That sentence had a bit of a bite to it, Julia," he said quietly. "You know you're just throwing more challenges at me. I want nothing more than to hold you in my arms, in my bed, and have you tell me you want my kisses." He slipped his hand behind her neck and caressed her nape. "And it's going to happen. You'll be mine."

"Nick! Dream on at your own risk," she exclaimed.

"I'll take that chance."

"Let's try a safer subject. Tell me some more about the quarter horses," she said, trying to pay attention while he talked. He leaned closer and his fingers tangled in her hair and caressed her nape, feathery strokes fueling her desire.

They talked, argued, teased. Time passed, and she had to admit she could too easily continue chatting with him the rest of the night. Effortlessly, Nick charmed and beguiled.

She took his wrist and looked at his watch. "Nick, it's after three in the morning!" she exclaimed, standing. "I think I should turn in," she said. The night was over, but Nick had stirred her up and her nerves were raw. Even at this hour, she knew she wouldn't sleep. She wanted him desperately.

She pulled her hand away from his and stood. He came to his feet at once.

"Then I'll walk you to your room."

She laughed. "All twenty steps with me? I can find my way."

He placed his arm across her shoulders. "I want to be with you as long as possible," he said seductively.

His warm body was close beside hers and he smelled of a tangy, inviting aftershave. His arm tightened and he pulled her closer against him.

"When I said we should get to know each other better, this isn't what I had in mind," she stated, trying to ignore her tingly awareness.

"It's exactly what I had in mind and I think it's grand," he said.

They walked along the deck, moving in the moonlight and then they were in the shadow of the pilothouse. It was darker, the passageway more narrow. Nick stopped and turned to face her, resting his hands on her waist. "It's been a good day, Julia. Better than I ever thought possible."

As she looked up at him she placed her hands on his forearms. "Nick, there's an invisible line that I don't want to cross."

"You know I'm going to kiss you. Sooner or later," he said quietly in a low drawl, and her heartbeat quickened. "I don't like later. I want now." His face was in shadow and she couldn't see his dark eyes, but she knew he watched her, and she imagined the intensity of his gaze.

"We need space between us, Nick."

"Why? We agreed no business. It's just a man and a woman. You and I have been headed this way since the dog ran in front of my car in the parking lot."

Her heart thudded as Nick drew her into his arms. He leaned down and brushed a kiss on her lips. Featherlight, yet his warm lips melted her.

"Nick," she whispered, but her protest faded as his mouth closed on hers. When his tongue slipped into her mouth, playing over her tongue, every stroke shot fiery sparks through her. Sliding his arm around her waist, he drew her closer.

All she was aware of was him, his strong arm circling her waist, his lips on hers, his tongue in her mouth. With the first slight contact, caution took wing and flew away.

As she pressed more fully against his long, hard length, his arm tightened around her. Bending over her and holding her close, Nick flexed his powerful muscles. She ached to devour this vital, sexy male.

His kiss consumed her while she shook with passion. Desire flared hot and low in her, and she thrust her hips against him.

All their touches, the flirting, the feathery contacts and double entendres burst into thundering longing. He had her primed and ready for his kiss, yet she dimly realized that she also had a devastating effect on him.

His thick, hard shaft pressed hotly against her. Wanting to demolish him as much as he destroyed her, she wound one arm around his neck and she rubbed against him, slowly.

While her pulse raced, he gasped for breath, a tremor shaking him. His passionate kisses demanded her response, and her need for more of him built rapidly.

She had guessed accurately that his kisses would be devastating. Each stroke of his tongue sent her pulse galloping. Just his kisses set off fireworks inside her. She responded, kissing him while moving seductively against him and wanting him more than she had thought possible.

She moaned with pleasure, the sound lost in his kiss. Stroking his muscled back, she relished the hard feel of him against her. A sheen of sweat covered his smooth, warm skin.

As he wound his other hand in her hair, he pulled her head back so he could kiss her.

Standing in his arms, kissing him, was a dream come true, or was it a nightmare unfolding? She wanted his kisses, but at the same time she realized that she had opened Pandora's box of problems.

She leaned away to run her hands across his chest, sliding them slowly over sculpted muscles. Delighting in him, she tangled her fingers in the thick mat of curly hair across his chest.

Then he wrapped her in his embrace, leaned over her, molding her against him as he kissed her. Arching up against him, she clung and returned his kisses, hoping she overwhelmed him as he did her. She wanted to set him on fire, make him remember her, be more than just another woman for him to conquer.

Releasing her pent-up hunger, she let passion run riot. Her fiery response to his sex appeal mixed with her anger over his arrogance and ambition.

For this moment, like sunshine on fog, their kisses burned away the discord between them. Desire consumed her and she wanted him as she had never wanted a man before. At this instant, Nick was special, the most exciting man on earth, and, her hunger to hold and kiss him overcame judgment.

Passion escalated with breathtaking swiftness. Far too fast, desire flamed.

As she explored him, his hands slipped up from her waist to touch the underside of her breasts. His fingers brushed across her breasts, so lightly, yet his touch was a white-hot brand. She gasped with pleasure, catching his wrists and pulling his hands down. "No," she whispered.

Pushing against him, she turned her head. On fire with wanting him, she gasped for breath. While her entire body tingled, she wanted to go right back into his embrace, but she knew better than to do so. "We stop now," she said hoarsely, unable to resist drawing her fingers across his rock-hard chest.

She shouldn't have ever let things get as out of hand between them, but she liked kissing him, liked it too much. She wanted to make love to him and have him love her in return. And that could be something that could wreck and destroy too much in her life in the future. Regret threatened to be enormous.

"We traveled where we don't belong. There's no forgetting the enormous differences between us."

"The differences lie in business," he whispered, leaning forward to brush kisses along her throat. "They have nothing to do with us right now. I can keep work and pleasure separate."

She stepped back out of his embrace. The rail was at her back as she gazed up at him and placed her hands on both sides of his face

"Nick, it isn't business and pleasure—it's lifestyles and values. We each measure success differently. To you, it's money and acquisitions and a career. I value love and family and lasting relationships. We're worlds apart. You know we can't separate our personal lives and what we hold worthy."

"It's just kisses, Julia," he replied quietly while he caressed her throat.

"We can't resolve the friction between us with kisses. I don't want to get emotionally involved and compound our battle. And it is a battle. You know that without hearing it from me," she added.

"Are you trying to convince me or yourself?" he asked softly, tucking a tendril of her hair behind her ear.

"Maybe both of us," she admitted. "We both know there is chemistry between us."

"A damn hot one," he said in that seductive drawl that made her knees weak. "It's a weekend together. Relax, enjoy it, some dancing, some kisses—don't be so uptight about them. I'm not propositioning you. C'mon, lighten up."

"I don't want to fall in love with you," she stated bluntly. Anger heated her that he would so blithely pass off the attraction between them. His statement reinforced her determination to resist his charms.

"I didn't say one word about anyone falling in love," he said quietly. "We can have a wonderful, intimate relationship—"

"Not I, Nick!" she snapped. "There's no such thing as a wonderful, intimate relationship without love. That's a hollow, empty life."

"You're missing out on some great moments, Julia," he said

in a velvety rasp that was seduction all by itself. "Don't take life so seriously."

"As if you don't take it seriously when you lose a business deal. And you occasionally have lost, haven't you, Nick? Somewhere back in the history of Ransome, you've lost?"

Anger flashed but was gone so swiftly from his expression that if she hadn't known him as well as she did now, she wouldn't have caught it. She knew she had struck a nerve—he not only took losing seriously, he loathed it and didn't want to acknowledge it.

"When did you lose last, Nick?" she asked softly, unable to resist needling him but fully aware that she was toying with a tiger that had incredibly sharp claws. "How civilized and light-hearted were you then?"

He stepped closer, wound his fingers in her hair and tilted her head back. He was breathing heavily and anger burned in his brown eyes. "You're pushing me and you know it. You're doing it deliberately."

"You're the one who said to lighten up and not take life so seriously," she reminded him, hoping he couldn't hear her pounding heartbeat or realize how much she wanted to kiss him. He was after her body and she wasn't going to satisfy him because she knew he had no interest in her heart. His love was making deals, power and financial success.

He inhaled and leaned down, tightening his arm around her to pull her tightly against him. "You're going to be mine. We've got this fire and it's too rare to ignore. Sometime soon, you're going to stop being cautious and careful and throw yourself into life just the way you threw yourself in front of my car to protect that dog. All this caution isn't your natural self. And the more you goad me, the more I'm coming after you, Julia. The more you challenge me, the more I intend to seduce. You've had your warning."

"So do you always get your way? I don't think so, Nick. And this is one time you won't. You want my body. You practice seduction and chase success. Just beware, that you don't discover there are other values more important in life. Mess with me and you'll proceed at your own risk," she warned him.

He gave her a mocking smile. "I'll remember your warning and take my chances. And I'll start now." He hauled her close suddenly and bent to kiss her hard and long.

His kiss electrified her, demolishing her ability to coolly stand back and merely observe what he was doing.

She kissed him in return, her tongue stroking his with the same fury that he had given her. When he leaned over her, she tightened her arms around his neck.

"You'll be mine, Julia," he vowed. He ducked his head to kiss her hard, silencing any answer she might have given him.

With her thoughts spinning, she held him while she arched her hips against him. Purpose and resolutions vanished. There was only Nick and his devastating kisses. Desire pounded in her, hot demanding, her body craving more.

They were locked in battle and she knew it was too late to turn back. She leaned away and opened her eyes. "This is one fight you won't win, Nick," she whispered.

"Yes, I will," he answered and then kissed her and silenced her. He drove thoughts of competition, threats and warnings out of mind. She kissed him recklessly, wanting him wildly.

She slid her hand down his back to his waist, feeling his smooth back, and then let her hand slide down his hip. She heard a growl in his throat. He tightened his arm around her, and his thick rod pressed against her.

He set her ablaze, but his response to her was evident, too. She could feel his arousal, as well as the tremors that shook him and the damp sweat on his skin. His breath was as ragged as hers. His kisses this time around were more fiery than last time.

His hand tugged her T-shirt out of her shorts and he slid his fingers up over her ribs. Then his large hand cupped her breast through her bra and his thumb played back and forth lightly over her nipple.

She gasped with pleasure, her desire escalating in quantum leaps. He slipped his fingers beneath her bra.

She caught his hand, opening her eyes slowly, dazed and aching with need. "Now we stop, Nick. I'm not getting on your yacht and falling into your arms and into your bed within hours of sailing."

"You like my hands on you, Julia," he said softly as he nuzzled her neck and ran his hand lightly down her back and over the curve of her bottom.

She twisted away. "I'm calling it a night," she announced. She hated her breathless voice for giving away the effect he'd had on her. His gaze traveled over her and she was aware of her taut nipples pushing against the cotton fabric of her T-shirt. Her pulse pounded and she ached for more of him.

"I'll walk you to your cabin."

"No need for that," she replied dryly. "I couldn't possibly get lost. You know I've had a good time, Nick. Far too good."

"Admit it, Julia," he said, stepping closer and touching the neckline of her shirt. "The evening was hot, sexy and exciting. Wasn't it?"

"You just have to hear me admit it, don't you? All right, Nick. You're sexy and you're exciting. The day and night have been fabulous," she admitted, watching him draw a deep breath and realizing her words were fueling his desire as much as caresses would have. "My heart is pounding. I'm breathless, on fire and I doubt if I'll sleep because of you and your incredible body. There. I said it. I'll see you in the morning."

He caught her arm and hauled her into his arms again. "How do you expect me to let you walk away when you tell me things like that?"

"Easily, Nick. I didn't tell you one thing you didn't already know and you pushed me to tell you. 'Night."

She wriggled free and hurried away from him without looking back. Her heart beat swiftly and she could feel his heated gaze as strongly as his consuming lust. She could imagine him debating silently with himself about coming after her.

Then she was shut away in her cabin, and she let out her breath. Her image in the mirror showed her tousled hair, her erect nipples, her red mouth that was rosier from his kisses. She ached with wanting him and wondered how she would sleep even an hour in the short time that was left of the night.

In spite of knowing full well that it was merely lust and determination to best her in business that motivated him, she liked being with him. He was an exciting, desirable man who could charm and kiss and captivate. If only—as always, she stopped that thought immediately.

She needed to constantly remember that Nick was after something she had. His lust and seductive ways had no effect on his heart. Women were objects of lust to him and that was all.

Moving automatically, Julia finally climbed into her bunk to stay awake, thinking about Nick, wanting him and lecturing herself. If she had good sense, she would go home tomorrow. She hadn't accomplished one thing and swaying Nick to her cause looked hopeless. The man seemed as stubborn as the proverbial mule.

She turned over, closed her eyes and tried to forget him, willing sleep to come. Instead, all she could think about was dancing with him, kissing him, flirting with him.

She had warned him to beware of losing his heart, but her heart was the one in jeopardy. Nick's pleasure was beating a competitor. Ambitious, out to win for the sake of winning, ruthless—all described Nick and she should remind herself of that constantly.

She stirred and woke with sun streaming in the portholes. For a moment, she was disoriented, but then she remembered where she was. She sat up and stretched and stood to get ready for another day with Nick.

Half an hour later, she found him cooking breakfast in the galley. Tempting smells of bacon and coffee wafted in the air. As she entered the galley, Nick set down a pot and it clanged lightly.

"Good morning," she said and he turned abruptly. For an instant, there was a flash of anger in his expression. Just as it had happened in his office, it was gone immediately and she wondered if she had imagined it both times. Why would he be furious now?

Five

As soon as she said good morning to him, Nick's pulse quickened. Her big blue eyes burned like a flame. Momentarily, his anger vanished. He forgot deals and rigs and business and threats. Desire blazed, hot and intense.

When she faced him, her eyes widened and she scanned his features. She tossed her head and her hair swung over her shoulder.

"What's wrong, Nick? You're solemn and quiet this morning."

He barely heard her question. When had he wanted a woman with this heart-pounding, breath-stopping intensity? He reached out to take her arm and closed the distance between them as he slid his other arm around her waist. Her eyes widened and then he looked at her mouth. When he did, her lips parted and she tilted her head back.

His heart thudded in his chest. To know that she felt what he did carried its own excitement.

She half closed her eyes and wound her arm around his neck.

"I want you, Julia," he whispered. "And you want me to kiss you."

"You're a danger to me. Because of business, we should keep our distance. Yet you are a temptation," she said, drawing out her words. She stood on tiptoe and pressed her mouth against his. With a groan, he slipped his arm around her tiny waist, marveling how she could look so small and fragile, yet be so sexy and strong. And her mouth was soft, sending molten fire down his insides, along his veins and into the center of his being. He leaned over her, kissing her hard while he tangled his fingers in her hair.

She clung to his shoulders and arched up beneath him. When her hips shifted against him, he slid his hand down the length of her from her throat, lightly, slowly over her breast, brushing her nipple that was taut and pointy. His hand slipped down over her hip and then along her thigh.

Her body pressing against his made him rock-hard. Mere anticipation aroused him. She kissed him while she combed her fingers in his hair. Then she wriggled away, her breasts rising and falling as she gulped for air.

"You're going too fast again."

"Seems to me you're the one who started this."

"I might have been," she admitted with a sly, coaxing smile that made him want to pull her right back into his embrace. "I'll help get breakfast while you tell me what's bothering you."

He turned to fix toast, debating whether to share his news with her. "I had some e-mails from Tyler that were about business deals that have problems. I didn't know my feelings were showing."

She placed one hand on her hip and studied him. "So is one of the problems Holcomb Drilling?"

Again, he was tempted to tell her the truth, to let her know the reason for his fury. But it was his nature to keep things to himself and he clamped his lips closed. "This morning, my e-mails were far removed from Holcomb Drilling," he said, knowing there was nothing yet that revealed with certainty that Holcomb people had any part in the rig fire. But now, from Tyler's messages, Nick knew that the oil rig fire had been deliberately set. Tyler had made it clear that the investigator didn't have any leads yet on the arsonist, but the authorities had fingerprints now, as well as a picture from a security camera of a man running across the rig. With so much evidence, they hoped they could identify the criminal.

Nick had no doubt the information would lead back to Rufus Holcomb. Or maybe Julia herself. She had threatened him and she could have easily given the orders.

She set out orange juice and glasses and mugs.

He watched her moving around the galley as she poured coffee and a tumbler of orange juice. She was graceful and sexy in her movements.

In spite of his anger, the feud between their families and the possibility she was behind the rig sabotage, he wanted Julia more than he could recall wanting any woman.

Even if there hadn't been all those differences between them, they clashed because they both were strong-willed. If they got into any kind of relationship, even briefly, he knew her goal would be marriage while his would be gratification and enjoyment. The satisfaction of lust and the pleasure of each other's company were sufficient for him. He didn't want permanent commitment. He couldn't cope with it.

Forgetting his problems, he watched her and he wiped his damp brow. The temperature was rising. He knew it was the direction of his thoughts about her that had him sweating. She had a more intense effect on him than other women did. He was surprised by his reaction, because he didn't want her to stir him so easily.

When his gaze ran down her long, shapely legs, his pulse climbed another notch. Her silky blond hair fell freely over her shoulders. She wore cutoffs and a short blue cami that left a bare midriff. Her cutoffs hugged her hips and rode low beneath her navel, revealing her flat stomach.

The cami had spaghetti straps and lace across the low neckline. More enticing bare skin and luscious curves were revealed. He studied her appreciatively. She was the best-looking woman he had ever known. And the sexiest. Too bad she was from a family that his had feuded with through three generations. Even worse, she was so tied up in family and marriage. Otherwise, what a time they could have!

Still, he intended to have a damn fine time with her anyway. It just wouldn't last as long as he wanted because the time to deal with Holcomb was looming, and then she would be furious with him forever after. He was going to take Rufus's company and enjoy doing it. He wasn't going to ruin the old man, but Julia would never view the purchase of their business as anything except evil, no matter how much money she got from the buyout. Drawing a deep breath, Nick controlled the urge to take her in his arms and kiss her until he could carry her to bed. He was certain he could seduce her.

Who was the man in her life? Nick wondered. She had said none and maybe she truly was like he was—and hadn't been seeing anyone lately, but he couldn't imagine that. She was far too beautiful, far too sexy to sit home alone at night.

He look at the slight sway of her hair as she walked around the galley. He could watch her all day because she was fascinating to him. He wanted to reach for her now and forget cooking and breakfast. He wanted to get right to his plans for the day—her seduction.

She stopped to pour two mugs of coffee.

Walking over to her, Nick stood close behind her and inhaled her perfume, smelling the clean, soapy scent of her hair. He placed his hands on her shoulders. She glanced over her shoulder at him and smiled. His heartbeat quickened.

"Maybe we should skip breakfast," he said. His voice had thickened and he let his desire for her show. He slid his hands slowly down her arms to her elbows and then back up again to her shoulders. Her skin was smooth and warm, silky to his touch.

Her expression changed as she inhaled and turned to face him. "Great minds think alike. Or something like that," she said, her voice trailing away. She placed her hand behind his head, winding her fingers in his hair, and he had to draw a shaky breath.

She got that hot, lethargic glaze in her eyes that excited him. She stood on tiptoe, pulled his head down and kissed him.

Instantly, he wrapped his arms around her and his mouth came down hard on hers. He let go his pent-up longing and kissed her passionately, wanting her naked now but knowing he had to wait. His blood pounded hotly in his veins. He wondered if he could ever get enough of her. When they made love, he vowed silently that it would be long, slow, thorough. He wanted to take forever to kiss and caress her. He wanted her softness wrapped all around him, enveloping him.

She was the most exciting woman he had ever known and it surprised him. So far, her hot kisses burned him to cinders and she responded passionately to his kisses.

As he kissed her, he inhaled, shaking with his effort to control the urge to start peeling her out of her clothes. He had to take time, to take care, he reminded himself, but he wanted her and she was driving him wild. His blood thundered hotly through his veins.

"Julia," he whispered, wrapping his arms around her tightly to kiss her. He needed her softness and her sweetness. He wanted her fire. She took his breath away with her beauty and sexiness.

His need compounded swiftly, a hot flame low between his legs. He throbbed with desire, aching while he tried to maintain his control. Her softness pressed against him, burning him like a brand. He wound one hand in her hair. He leaned away to pull the cami over her head, tossing it aside. His breath caught as he looked at her lush breasts.

With a raspy breath he leaned back and cupped her breasts in his hands. She was soft, warm, burning him. He groaned as he leaned down to take her breast in his mouth and his tongue circled her nipple. He heard her moan, felt her fingers winding in his hair.

Her waist was incredibly tiny. She felt fragile, so dainty, yet he knew from swimming with her that she was far from delicate. How could she be so tiny, yet so strong? Her body amazed him. Her breasts were full, beautiful, and his pulse thundered in his ears as he drew his tongue over her nipple again.

"Nick!" she gasped and clung to him.

She straightened and caught his hands, moving them and then turning to yank up her clothes.

Her back was to him and he stepped close behind her, sliding his arms around her while his tongue traced the curve of her ear. He whispered in her ear, "I want you. I want to shower kisses all over you from your head to your toe. I want to see what makes you respond and what drives you wild with passion."

She stopped his words, kissing him as if he were the last man on earth and this was the last kiss. He groaned, but the sound was lost in her kisses.

He unfastened the waist of his cutoffs and then she caught his hands. She gasped for breath as she stepped back.

"Nick. Slow down. We barely know each other. We're going to be enemies in a few days—"

"No, we're not, Julia. Not in a few days, not ever," he said, knowing that his fury with her was temporarily banked, but it would return. Yet at this moment, he couldn't imagine staying angry with her. All he wanted was her in his arms. "I have to love you, darlin'. Make love to every beautiful inch of you," he murmured. "The sooner we do, the more time we'll have—"

"Shh, Nick," she said softly, placing her finger on his mouth. "Hush! We're not making love. We've kissed too much already. I don't live like you do, love like you do. I can never be casual about a physical relationship."

He smiled at her, listening to her protests, yet watching the vein in her throat pulse at an accelerated rate. She was breathless. Her nipples were taut. Her lips looked swollen, ready for more kisses. "We will make love, Julia. I promise you. After the kisses we've shared, I'm not walking away and neither are you. Our kisses promise fiery sex beyond all imagination. I'm not letting that escape me and you won't, either."

"You slow down," she argued, stepping back while her eyes remained locked with his. She moved slowly, carefully. She desired him. He saw it in her blue eyes, knew it from her kisses. She was fighting yielding to her desire, but he was certain she wanted to make love as badly as he did.

He knew she was scared of his motives and she had good reason to be. Yet she was a strong woman and knew what she wanted. He wouldn't be taking advantage of anyone because she would never let him.

Turning her back, she slithered into her cami. As she crossed the galley, she straightened her clothes and drank some of her orange juice. She set down the glass and studied him from a distance. He turned to put on eggs, making an omelet. As she watched him flip the omelet, she spoke up.

"Nick, something's bothering you. What is it?"

She surprised him. He didn't think he ever let his feelings show. He couldn't remember anyone else knowing when something was bothering him unless he wanted that person to know. He paused and gave her a level look. She stared back unflinchingly.

"I heard from Tyler. The rig fire was deliberately set."

"How awful! Do they—" She stopped abruptly and her eyes widened. "You still think we did it, don't you?"

"Who else has threatened me within the month?"

"I can't imagine, but no one from Holcomb has done anything to your blasted rig. You're way too suspicious, Nick!"

Her blue eyes blazed and she caught her lower lip in her even white teeth while she stared at him. His anger heightened because he was absolutely certain that Holcomb people were behind the fire.

"C'mon, Julia. You have no idea what your granddad has ordered. You swear you weren't involved in any way?"

His question hung in the air. Her face flushed and she glared at him.

"I swear I was not!" She ground out the words. "I know you want to blame us since Granddad and I both threatened you, but that wasn't the kind of threat I was making and neither was he. You know we aren't behind setting your rig on fire or any other sabotage to your company!"

Nick walked up to her. Her eyes were clear and her gaze steady. If she was lying, she was damn good at it. But he had been lied to before in a very convincing manner and he wasn't going to be taken in now by big blue eyes and a beautiful face. He slipped his hand behind her head.

"All right, I'll accept that, but if I find out you or your granddad were behind it, I'll destroy Holcomb bit by bit."

She shrugged. "That means nothing to me, Nick. We didn't set your fire so that's the end of it."

He looked down into her guileless expression and wondered if he could trust her. He would get to the truth. It was just a matter of time. Until then, he would try to curb his anger. But he was certain either Julia or her granddad or both were behind the fire. He was tempted to believe she really didn't know and it was just her granddad, but he wasn't going to be now, no matter how beautiful and beguiling she was.

"They'll find out who did it eventually. They have prints and our security camera caught a picture of a man running across the rig."

"Good. Then you'll know for sure."

"We'll see, Julia. I have a reward that ought to flush out the guilty party. Someone is going to be happy to tell what he knows."

"I hope you find out exactly who did it," she said. "In the meantime, if you're going to stay angry all day, there's little point in us continuing here. We might as well weigh anchor and go."

Amused, he relaxed and forgot business. "We're not going to weigh anchor yet. We have a beautiful day ahead of us. Let's have breakfast and swim and plan what we'll do." He leaned down. "I'll forget differences for now if you will," he coaxed and she nodded.

They ate leisurely and talked, avoiding the topic of business. Part of the time, he didn't even hear what she was telling him except he knew vaguely that it was about her years at college. His thoughts were on kissing her and peeling those clothes off her. Soon he was getting aroused by his imagination, so he tried to concentrate on what she was saying.

"This is paradise Nick. No cell phones—no phones. I don't have any electronic gadgets with me right now."

"I can see you don't," he said, looking her over slowly. Revenge couldn't possibly be sweeter than his would be. He had waited and worked for years, but had never dreamed it would involve the seduction of a drop-dead gorgeous woman who fascinated him. Yet once the buyout occurred, he was going to sever all chances of ever making love to her again.

The realization gave him pause for thought, but then he shrugged it away. He would forget her. There were other beauties in the world. Take away the sex, and he'd had a good time anyway, he had to admit it. She was good company, a great dancer, could swim, challenged him constantly and wasn't intimidated by him.

Nor was she dazzled by him as some women so obviously were. They wanted to please him at all costs. Julia would never be that way. Far from it.

For the first time, his thirst for revenge wavered. He didn't even know if she was involved. Surprising himself, he stared at her and realized he didn't want revenge to get in the way of a relationship with Julia.

An hour later, they sat on the deck in a light, early morning breeze. Nick wanted to reach for her again, but he curbed the impulse.

"It's beautiful out here," she murmured.

He glanced at her long, bare legs appreciatively. "It's gorgeous," he agreed.

She gave him a sharp look and then smiled at him. "Thanks, Nick," she said patiently. "The water is beautiful."

"You're thinking about it the way it was last night in the dark," he said quietly, surprised that she still had the fear from childhood. He doubted if she feared much else in life.

She shook her shoulders slightly. "I know. A silly fear, but one that I can't get rid of, although I did for a few moments last night. You made me forget it."

"When you say things like that to me, I want to take you in my arms and kiss you senseless," he said, his voice hoarse.

She placed her hand on his arm and his heart raced. "You stay right where you are," she said. She tilted her head to study him. "Last night, you said you feared losing. Why, Nick? What happened to you somewhere in your past that made you to lose so much? No one likes to lose, but most of us know we're going to lose off and on during our lifetime, so we accept it."

He thought about winning and losing and knew it ran deeper than that. And it was a subject he never talked about. It was one he didn't like to think about.

"You still don't have to like it when you lose, just because it happens once in a while," he said lightly.

"I'll bet it's happened very little to you."

"It happens," he said and looked away.

There was a steady slap of small waves against the hull, a reminder that they were on water.

"Sorry, I shouldn't have asked you a personal question," she said quietly, and he turned to look at her.

She had her lower lip caught in her teeth, and she shrugged. "How much time do you spend on your ranch?" she asked and he knew she was trying to steer the conversation away from the topic of losing. He thought about why he hated losing. He had hated it all his life.

"You can ask me about losing." He stared beyond her, remembering moments when he was a child, remembering hurts and longings. "As a kid when I did, Dad made me miserable. And I never could please him, no matter what I won. I've never been able to be good enough for him."

"That can't be true now since you're grown," Julia said. "You've built Ransome Enterprises into a much larger company. I know you have made some terrific deals. I know you have more than a few trophies from riding in rodeos. You have a reputation for succeeding at everything you do."

"It's still not good enough," Nick said, feeling old hurts stir and knowing he was foolish to let his father and childhood hurts get him down.

"I can't believe that!" she exclaimed, leaning forward to put her hand on his. He forgot about the conversation momentarily.

"That's awful," she said. "My whole family always praised me—often far more than I deserved, but I knew they approved of me all my life. It would be dreadful to never get that approval from a parent."

He picked up her hand to brush a light kiss across her knuckles.

"Don't stare at me like I just announced I've been an orphan and living on the streets. Of course, I'm happy to have your sympathy and attention," he said, lowering his voice and picking her hand up again to rub along his jaw.

She let him and he realized she was feeling sorry for him and allowing him more liberties because of her sympathy.

"I can't believe you've grown up that way," she said.

"Well, I did. Maybe I'm the proverbial 'middle child.' Dad always threw Matt up to me as so successful—Matt could ride broncs better, throw a ball better."

Nick brushed kisses lightly along her knuckles and then turned her hand and let his tongue play in her palm. His thumb was on her wrist and he felt her pulse race. She leaned toward him, listening to him talk as if what he was saying was the most important thing she'd ever heard.

"For years Matt was bigger because we were growing boys and I was younger. It was always something," Nick said.

"That's dreadful! You've been far more successful than your father was."

"Maybe not in his eyes. I don't ever remember high praise from him. He praised Matt and he adored Jeff. Those were the years when we were growing up and I was a year younger. Matt was the oldest son, the firstborn, able to do things before I could. Jeff was the youngest son, Dad's delight, the son he spoiled. Katherine is the only girl."

"You seem to get along with your brother now."

"I do. In the first place, Matt never worried about the competition. He was older and for years, he was bigger. Jeff was spoiled by Dad and he didn't worry about competing with either Matt or me.

"So that left me. Actually, for years it's been my dad, not Matt, that I've always wanted to best. When we were grown, I could beat Matt at some things, but I've always been driven to top Dad. The biggest way of all to surpass him is to do better in business. That used to get to him. Now that his health is poor and he's older, he's mellowed a degree, maybe. He's a tough one."

"Maybe he didn't know a lot about raising children."

"Probably didn't know a damn thing about it. He had no experience until he had us and then he had to raise us single-handedly. I competed with Dad, but then once I found I could make deals, I liked what I was doing and Dad was no longer a part of it. Or maybe not as big a part. Somewhere in me, there's always the son who wants to hear some praise from his father."

"Sounds as if you both are too much alike," she said, remembering Granddad telling her how Nick's father had threatened him on more than one occasion. She had heard him talk about the time they had a shouting match in a shopping center. She had already discovered that Nick was competitive in everything he did.

Nick shifted his focus back to her. "You're probably right. We're the most alike—aggressive, operating a little on the edge, determined and ambitious. Business is the most important aspect of what we are and do. Business defines us."

"Business and success," she replied. "Ah, Nick. You can't imagine what you're missing in life."

"Feel sorry for me?" he asked with amusement.

"No, I don't. You're conscious of your choice and doing what you want."

"You're right there. At the moment, I'm overwhelmed by a blonde who has the ability to make me forget everything else."

"I don't think so." She stood. "I think it's time to swim."

He suspected she wanted to get away from the intimate, personal conversation.

Smiling, he stood. "You don't have your suit on under those clothes. Are we skinny-dipping?"

"Absolutely not!" she snapped and left swiftly. He chuckled, watching her stride away, his pulse beating fast in anticipation of a day with her.

* * *

For an hour they swam and then Nick piled picnic provisions into a fiberglass dinghy and they rowed to the beach.

"Pick a spot and we'll have a picnic and tour the beach," he said.

He watched her look around. She was in her swimsuit with a black, sheer cover-up that still gave him an enticing view. He wore a T-shirt over his suit.

"There," she said, picking up an armload to help him carry their things to the palm she had selected. They spread a blanket and put everything down on it. He took her hand.

"It's too early to eat. Let's look around."

She was dazzled by the place while he was dazzled by her. He watched her, laughed with her. She had caught her hair up in a ponytail clipped behind her head. They wandered along the white beach beneath swaying palms, hearing the rustle of the fronds.

"This is so beautiful!" she said, touching a low-hanging frond and turning to look at him. "We should have known each other somewhere else, Nick. Some other time in life."

"Do I hear regrets?" he asked. She stood near a tall, graceful palm tree. He walked over to her and placed his hands on her shoulders.

"Yes. I have regrets because this weekend is turning out to be—" she paused a heartbeat "—a very good time," she finished, her gaze sliding away. He brushed a kiss on her cheek and then her temple.

"It doesn't have to end," he declared.

She smiled at him. "Yes, it'll end like smashing a glass."

"In the meantime, here we are with the day spreading before us and the best company possible for me. This is great, Julia. I want our friendship to last when we go back."

"We'll see."

"That's a no. Let's prolong what we have. We won't talk business until tomorrow. Another evening that is sexy and exciting and full of great feelings, fine food and terrific dancing. How about it, Julia?" he coaxed.

That's what he wanted. He had no interest in business this weekend. He no longer had interest in revenge. He was having a fabulous time with her, and he wanted another twenty-four hours like the past hours. He brushed a kiss on her throat.

"C'mon, say yes. Let me have my way. I'll try to make it an evening to remember," he whispered, his tongue tracing the curve of her ear. "Give me what I want."

She smiled up at him, a heated, sexy look that made his blood thicken. "I suspect you get too much of what you want all the time, Nick. Someone should say no to you."

"I get plenty of no's. And I don't want any from you, especially not now." He raised his head. "Look at this—we're in paradise and we have it all to ourselves. Palms, water, sunshine, perfect weather, privacy." He looked down at her and slid his arm around her waist, hauling her up against him to wrap his arms around her.

"Hot, steamy sex that you won't forget. See if I can't make your pulse pound."

"You know you can," she whispered.

He felt as if he were drowning in depths of blue as she looked wide-eyed at him. He leaned down to kiss her, his mouth covering hers and his tongue thrusting into her mouth.

She wrapped her arms around his neck and he caressed her throat, making her arch against him and tighten her arms. He leaned back and peeled away her flimsy cover-up and the top scrap of her swimsuit to cup her breasts.

He gave her a heavy-lidded, smoldering look and then lowered his attention. "You're gorgeous!" he murmured, cupping her breasts in his large hands, circling his thumbs over her nipples until he bent his head to take one taut bud in his mouth.

"Nick!" she gasped, winding her fingers in his hair while her other hand slid down, to caress his chest. Her fingers slid lightly over him and his heart pounded. He wanted her now, yet he wanted to savor their time together and make love for hours.

He kissed her throat. His tongue traced over her ear. "We're going to make love," he said softly in her ear. He brushed kisses along her throat. "I'm going to make you let go and love until passion is a raging fire."

He stepped back to look at her and slide his hands to her waist. "Now, Julia, now say yes to me. I want you to say yes."

Six

Julia barely heard him. Her heart pounded, and she opened her eyelids that suddenly felt heavy. She wanted Nick and from the first moment they'd met, desire had been burning brighter, hotter, a flame that licked along her veins and throbbed inside.

She ran her hands across his strong chest, feeling the sculpted, hard muscles, tangling her fingers in the mat of his chest hair while she was consumed by his dark stare.

She looked lower. Her gaze slid down across his powerful chest, and her hands drifted lightly to his narrow waist and then along his slim hips. She gasped when he cupped her breasts again and ran his thumb in lazy circles over each nipple. She moved her hips, wanting him, desperation building. She lost all sense of time and all arguments of logic that declared Nick off limits and dangerous territory.

Gone were the barriers, common sense, caution. They were replaced by a driving hunger that had built hourly. Desire filled her, burning away everything else. She wanted Nick to make love to her. She wanted to touch him and kiss him. She hooked her fingers in his narrow strip of swim trunks and tugged them down to free him.

Her pulse pounded as she gazed at him. He was muscled, aroused, tan and fit. His body was male perfection, and she leaned forward to trace her fingers across his chest.

He pulled away the bottom of her swimsuit and held her away from him, his eyes moving hotly over her, making her nerves tingle as much as if he had been running his fingers over her.

"Beautiful, darlin'. You're fantastic," he murmured. He leaned down to cup her breast and take her nipple in his mouth, sucking and running his tongue slowly over her pouty bud.

"Nick!" she gasped, closing her eyes and clinging to his waist, her hips moving as she pulled him to her. She knelt in the sand, moving down slowly and letting her tongue trail down over his flat, washboard stomach and then she took his hot shaft in her hand. With the tip of her tongue, she traced his thick rod up to the velvet tip, letting her warm breath drift over him, relishing his fingers tangling in her hair and his groans of pleasure.

"Like that?" she whispered. "And that? I want to pleasure you, to demolish you, to finish the storm you started when we met."

She took him into her mouth, running her tongue over him while her hand slid low between his legs and caressed him.

His hands went beneath her arms and he lifted her up. Desire made him heavy-lidded. His lips were wet and red from kisses and he was gasping for breath. He looked at her mouth, then wrapped her in his embrace and kissed her hard and long.

Kneeling in the sand, he lowered her easily and turned her over. "I'm going to touch and kiss every gorgeous inch of you. You're beautiful," he said softly, brushing feathery kisses on her ankle, then up over her calf to the back of her knee. His tongue drew lazy circles that were erotic and she tried to turn to reach for him, but his hand in the small of her back pushed gently.

"Let me kiss and love you," he cooed. His breath was tantalizing and warm behind her knee, another blaze igniting in her, adding to the wildfire.

Then he moved higher, his tongue drifting along the back of her thigh, his breath hot on her bare skin. His hands played over her naked bottom, stroking, teasing.

He straddled her and moved higher. By the time he kissed her nape and then her ear, she was moaning with desire. She turned over, reaching for him while he started again at her feet while his hands caressed her inner thighs.

Sensations bombarded her. She couldn't be still. She wanted him and he was building her need by the second.

She turned and sat up, pulling him to her to kiss him passionately while her hand went to his manhood and caressed him. Then she pushed him and leaned down to kiss and lick him again.

"I want you, Nick. I want you now," she said, pausing to look up at him. The desire in his gaze took her breath and then they were in each other's embrace and she felt his thudding heart pounding against hers.

As he leaned over her and she clung to him, kissing him back, one of his hands slid down her back. He shifted her, placing her back on the sand. He moved between her legs, lifting them over his shoulders to give him access to her.

She was drowning in need for him, wanting his lovemaking, gasping and stroking his thighs. Watching her steadily, he leaned forward, sliding his tongue over her intimately, finding her feminine bud, kissing and nipping and teasing until she was on fire and tugging at him, trying to get him to make love and end the exquisite torment.

He lowered her, pulling her close while his fingers went between her legs to rub her and stir a storm that drove every thought from mind.

There was no turning back now. She had to have Nick, all of him. They were on the sand in the sun, and she didn't care. She didn't know how private the cove was, if they would be alone.

But at the moment, nothing mattered except Nick—his irresistible body, his devastating hands, his possessive mouth. He was magic, hot sex, hard male.

"I want you," she choked out. She wanted him now and

wanted him to possess her, hot and hard and fast. "Nick," she urged, catching his arm. His fingers were still on her feminine bud, rubbing her and building a blaze.

Desire pounded with each of her heartbeats. She had to have release, had to have Nick! Clinging to him, she thrashed wildly to a sexual crescendo—higher, more urgent and then release that made her want all of him, not just his mouth and hands.

"Nick, love me," she said, opening her legs wide.

She pulled on him, and he moved between her legs. "Are you protected?" he asked, and she shook her head.

He stood, walked over to their picnic things and grabbed up his shorts to reach into a pocket. He returned, striding to her and she drew a deep breath as she looked at him. He was naked, virile, aroused. Strong, muscled and desirable beyond her wildest dreams.

She wanted him inside her. She wanted his hardness, his strength. And she wanted to make love to him in return. To drive him beyond rational thinking just as he had her.

With his gaze locked with hers, he knelt between her legs and opened the packet. She took the condom to put it on him until his shaking hands brushed hers lightly away.

"You're way too slow," he said hoarsely. "I want you more than I've ever wanted anyone," he admitted, and her heart pounded.

"If only that were true," she whispered. Oblivious of the warm sand beneath her, she watched him kneeling between her legs. He slid his hands lightly, slowly, along the inside of her thighs and she gasped, opening herself more to him. She raised her legs to lock them around his waist as she tried to draw him to her.

He was poised, ready, his shaft thick and hard. She stroked his thighs and watched while he lowered himself. Wrapping his arms around her, he kissed her. When he eased into her, she arched her hips and held him tightly.

Pausing, he raised his head, his eyes narrowing. "Julia—" His voice was hoarse.

She whispered, "I want you now."

"You're a virgin," he said flatly, starting to pull away.

Julia tightened her arms and legs around him and raised to kiss him, pulling him down again as she thrust her tongue into his mouth to kiss him passionately.

"Love me, Nick!" she demanded, tugging on him. He gave her one long, searching look before he groaned and then eased into her again. She held him tightly, kissing him, feeling a flash of pain that was gone as she moved with him.

"Julia!" he breathed and then returned to kissing her. They moved together, bonded, their rhythm increasing. She was lost to the moment, giving herself to him totally. Urgency drove them. Desire for him overwhelmed her, and sensations rocked her as she moved her hips with him.

Then he slowed, almost withdrawing, filling her. She cried out, tugging on him and arching against him. "Nick!" she gasped, her voice hoarse as she thrashed wildly beneath him.

And then he plunged hard and fast, and she spun off into a world of sensation.

Her climax burst in a release that blinded her. Within seconds, he shuddered as he thrust hard and cried her name again.

He pumped faster and she moved with him until he slowed and their ragged breathing began to return to normal.

Finally he lay still, his weight still held slightly off her. He scattered kisses over her face and then rose on his elbows to look down at her. "You should've told me you were a virgin."

"No," she said softly. "I know what I wanted." His dark eyes still blazed with desire, and he leaned down to kiss her long and passionately while she ran her fingers through his hair and kept her other arm wrapped tightly around him. His weight was heavy on her, but it was good and she liked holding him. Fleetingly, they were united, one together.

He turned on his side, keeping her with him as he stroked her hair away from her face and tucked strands behind her ear. "You're fabulous," he said and leaned forward to kiss her again.

She curled her arm around his neck and kissed him in return, a kiss of satisfaction. It was minutes before he leaned away. "I hope you know what you want."

"I do," she answered solemnly. "I know exactly," she said softly with more assurance than she truly felt. She had wanted him, badly enough to give herself to him physically in the most intimate way possible.

"You're gorgeous, sexy, enticing," he said, brushing kisses over her between each word.

"Thank you. You're not so bad yourself," she added, trying to keep the moment light, as much to convince herself that she hadn't committed her heart to him as to prove that any relationship between them would be casual and brief.

She ran her hands over him, delighting in his hard, muscled body. He was a marvel to her—fit, healthy and too sexy to resist.

"Next time will be better for you, I promise," he said.

"If we're in bed instead of hot sand, it'll be better," she teased.

"I could have gotten the blanket I brought for our picnic."

"Maybe next time," she said lazily, running her hands across his chest and tangling her fingers in the short hair on his chest.

"I've never made love to a virgin," he said, caressing her throat. "That's special, Julia."

"You didn't want to," she reminded him.

"I was surprised. And then I wanted you to be sure. I'm a little awed," he said solemnly, and she wondered what was running through his mind. He was making more of an issue about it than she had expected him to. "You're my woman now," he added.

"Yes, for now maybe, Nick. It's not a big deal."

"Yes it is, if you've waited this long. I'm amazed you've waited. You surprise me constantly."

"Maybe that's good."

He looked at her with so much warm satisfaction, her heart thudded. She couldn't imagine a groom looking at his bride with much more warmth and pleasure. She hugged him in return and kissed him lightly on the mouth.

"I have an idea," he said and she leaned back to look up at him. "Let's get back to the boat and satin sheets and comfort."

"Best idea you've had in the last two minutes," she said, smiling at him. He laughed and hugged her lightly.

He stood and pulled her up. She yanked on her swimsuit, turning to find him watching her. He walked to her silently, every step ratcheting up her pulse because of the hungry look in his eyes. He picked her up and carried her back to their picnic place. She wrapped her arms around his neck. At their basket, he set her on her feet and she turned, keeping her arm around his neck while she stood on tiptoe to kiss him. Desire fanned to life again, a fire licking along her veins, making her want him as if they hadn't just made love.

She kissed him passionately, wanting to steal his heart, afraid to study her own actions or probe too deeply yet about what she truly felt for him. Finally, she pushed against his chest.

"Let's get back to the boat," he said, gathering up their things. They loaded the dinghy and pushed off.

The sun was still high in the sky and once they had gotten their picnic things back on board his yacht, they spent the next hour languidly in bed until Nick talked her into a swim.

When she told him she was getting out, he swam closer and slipped his arm around her waist, pulling her to him so he could kiss her.

Her pulse hummed as she felt his hand caressing her, sliding over her back and bottom, up to her breasts to touch her nipples. She didn't know when he whisked away her suit or his, but she realized they were naked, pressed together in water deep enough that he held her and his feet probably barely touched the bottom.

He was warm, nude and wet, awakening her desire swiftly.

He raised his head. "C'mon. Let's get out," he said. His voice was gravelly, a rasp that conveyed his need for her had returned full-force.

She shut her mind to tomorrows or consequences, knowing she had never wanted a man as she did Nick. He climbed out and turned to lift her up onto the deck. He was wet, sunlight reflecting off tiny drops of water all over his shoulders and body, his face, everywhere. His hair was plastered to his scalp. Water still clung to his thick lashes.

He reached for her, drawing her to him to wrap his arms

around her and kiss her. His body was nude and warm, pressed against hers. He was aroused, and his thick shaft pushed hotly against her stomach. He picked her up and carried her to his large stateroom. A shaft of golden sunlight streamed through a porthole and spilled over the cabin. He stood her on her feet in the sunlight, holding her waist while his gaze traveled languidly over her.

"I want to kiss every gorgeous inch of you," he murmured.

He cupped her breasts in his hands. "So soft and warm," he whispered and bent to take a nipple in his mouth while he sucked and teased.

Sensations raced from his touch, fanning out to set every nerve ablaze. She quivered with wanting him, reaching for him and running her fingers over him.

She caressed him, her fingers drifting over hard muscles down along his strong thighs. She knelt to take him into her mouth, letting her tongue slide over him until he groaned and hauled her up to kiss her thoroughly.

"Nick," she sighed, astounded at how intensely she wanted him when they had just made love earlier. Yet his body dazzled her, and his hands and mouth set her ablaze.

He framed her face with his hands, looking at her solemnly. "You can't ever guess how much I want you."

She knew she would remember the moment forever. "Oh, Nick, if only…" He kissed her and her words were lost, but she wouldn't have finished her sentence because loving forever wasn't Nick's intention.

He picked her up again to carry her to his broad bunk, where he placed her down gently. Then he turned her and began showering slow kisses and feathery caresses, teasing and tantalizing, until she was quivering and tugging on him.

"Love me, Nick!" She pushed him down to straddle him, playing with his flat male nipples, letting her fingers flit over his chest while he caressed her breasts and then slipped his hands between her legs to rub and tease and find her erotic hidden places.

She gasped with pleasure throwing her head back, giving him access to her, yielding to the sensations that held her in their grip. She moved her hips until she leaned down to kiss him.

He rolled her over and reached out to get protection. Sunlight streamed across the center of the bunk, splashing over Nick and giving golden highlights to the bulge of his muscles. Her pulse raced as she watched him he put on a condom and move between her legs.

"This time we'll go slow and take our time."

As their eyes locked, she wrapped her long legs around him, pulling him to her. At this moment, he made her feel as if she were the most desirable woman on earth. His dark gaze burned into her, hot, eager, hungry. She tingled, aching and wanting him as she ran her hands over his slender hips, feeling the jutting bones. Then he leaned down to kiss her and she closed her eyes, wrapping her arms and holding him tightly.

He thrust slowly into her. Hot and thick, he filled her.

Her blood thickened, pounded, burning through her veins while she moved her hips.

He withdrew just as slowly, entering her again, taking his time, Again and again he repeated slow thrusts until she was wild, thrashing and tugging on him, need building and thundering in her ears.

Finally he moved, fast and hard. She cried out as lights exploded behind her closed lids while she climaxed. Ecstasy enveloped her, and she rocked with him until he climaxed and slowed.

"Julia, Julia," he murmured her name softly. She barely heard him and then he rolled over, keeping her with him so he could face her while he smiled at her again.

"It's good between us. All that it promised to be. I want to keep you here in my arms for the rest of our time together."

"That's not possible," she whispered.

"I'm going to make you want the same thing," he said, drawing his fingers along her arm. "I don't want to let you go."

"You'll change your mind when your stomach starts growling with hunger," she said in amusement. But his words thrilled her even though she knew she shouldn't give them much credence in the aftermath of passion.

His dark brown eyes searched her gaze and he studied her solemnly. Brown curls were damp on his forehead, and she pushed them back slightly.

"Julia, I want to keep seeing you. Go out with me Monday night," he said gazing solemnly at her.

She placed her finger on his lips. "Shh. We're worlds apart, Nick, in what we want."

"Ah, that business deal—"

"Not that," she said, interrupting him. "A year from now, that won't even be an issue. I'm talking about lifetime differences, our values and goals. Lifestyles."

"I just want you to go to dinner with me Monday night," he said tightly.

"No, you don't," she said, tracing her forefinger along his jaw. "You want more than Monday night. A vast chasm stands between us. You have your future mapped out and know what you want, and it's definitely not what I want in any man I get deeply involved with," she replied and her insides clenched. Was she so certain she wanted to toss his offer aside?

He stroked her face. "So you're just waiting for Mr. Right to come along?"

"Hardly. And don't worry, Nick. I know you're not into long commitments of any sort. No. If he does, then I want marriage and family. But that doesn't always work out and if it doesn't, I'll find a way to work with children. There are endless volunteer things I can do."

"And I'm sure there has never been a dearth of guys wanting to take you out," he said with a gruffness that surprised her. She couldn't imagine a shred of jealousy in Nick. "I'll bet you've already turned down proposals."

"I'm particular and I've never found anyone that I wanted to live with the rest of my life."

"'The rest of my life' sounds like a hell of a long time."

She laughed. "You talk about it as if it were a prison sentence.

With the right person, it will be the most wonderful relationship possible." She traced her finger through the hair on his chest and then slid her hand down over his bony hip and his muscled thigh.

"See what you do to me with just the slightest touch," he said, leaning down to kiss her throat.

"You can't want to make love again!" she exclaimed and then kissed him. His answer was lost as she wrapped her arms around his neck and he rolled over, pulling her on top of him while they kissed.

They explored each other, long and slow and leisurely. She didn't think about his offer or the future. She took today and knew that that was all she could be concerned about. Tomorrow was for later, when she could think clearly.

This time, she straddled him and he pulled her down on his thick shaft and she moved with him as urgency built to the same blinding, white-hot need that sent her spiraling into space with rockets exploding inside her. He rolled her over suddenly and reached his climax as he pumped into her. "I want you. You're mine, Julia. You belong to me now."

"And you belong to me, Nick," she whispered back. "This moment we've given to each other without holding back. Make love to me, Nick!"

She felt his shuddering release and then she was enveloped in his embrace as he turned on his side and pulled her close, wrapping his legs with hers and running his hand down her side. "Fantastic long legs," he said, caressing her leg.

His seduction had been intoxicating. She marveled over it. She never wanted to be out of his arms, but she knew that was impossible.

Just as impossible as a long-term relationship with him. Their family differences loomed large, but she knew that was just the tip of an iceberg of differences that would separate them forever. Even so, she wanted to make love with Nick. She had waited, hoping to wait for marriage, for one particular man who was incredibly special. She had found the one particular man who was special—he just wouldn't be part of her future.

She leaned forward to kiss Nick's throat and then lay back in his arms and looked at him. "You're special, Nick. Very special."

He pulled her close against him and they lay side by side. "Tell me what you want in life besides family and kids."

"I want it all, I guess," she admitted quietly. "I want to get Holcomb back making solid profits and in the black and keep it running for Granddad until he retires. Actually, keep it going as long as he lives. I want to do my accounting, what I've been trained to do. I want to spend time with my family, too. I want at least three children. I want to live right where I do now or near there, but that's because of Granddad."

"I want to see you and have you in my life. I want to take you to the opera, the rodeo, bring you back here with me. Instead of going to Santa Fe, we could come again next weekend. If you'll agree to come, I'll clear my schedule."

She shook her head. "Sorry. I don't think it's wise for us to plan any long-term time together."

He raised up to look at her, turning on his side and propping his head on his hand. "You mean it, don't you? You're not going to come back here with me anytime in the future, are you?"

"You won't care, Nick. There'll always be someone else," she answered lightly, but it stung her to tell him. She wound her fingers in locks of his hair and then drew her hand along his jaw and felt the short stubble of his beard. "You and I want different things so we'll go in different directions."

She pulled his head down to kiss him to stop the trend of the conversation.

Later, Nick grilled shrimp kabobs and they ate on deck while they watched the sun slip beneath the horizon. They danced until they drifted back to Nick's stateroom where they made love far into the night.

Nick fell asleep holding Julia in his arms. She lay on her side and watched the steady rise and fall of his chest. Her gaze traveled beyond him as she looked around the stateroom. Now moonlight spilled through the portholes and gave a silvery illumination to her surroundings. When her attention returned to Nick, her pulse drummed. They had loved most of the day and night. In a few hours, it would be dawn again.

Julia wished she could hold back the dawn and delay the intrusion of the world and problems and differences. She wanted to say yes to Nick's offers. She wanted badly to be with him and the thought of spending next weekend the same way as she had this one tore at her heart. Everything inside her screamed at her to accept.

If she continued to see him and it developed into a long-term relationship, Nick might fall in love with her.

She had to laugh at herself. How many women had succumbed to his charms with that very same reasoning, she wondered. Nick would always be Nick, and that meant single, center of his own world, steeped in ambition and driven to succeed and compete.

Not what she wanted in her life. Why did she have to keep reminding herself of that? His offers were pure temptation of the strongest kind. He was sexy, charming, everything she had suspected he would be when she had first encountered him in the restaurant parking lot.

He was so handsome it made her knees weak, and she could look at him for hours on end. He was so sexy, he had melted all her resistance and gotten past every barrier that had protected her heart all these years.

She wanted to continue to see him and she ached to have him in her life. She wanted to go with him on his travels, watch him ride in a rodeo. And she knew she couldn't do any of it. As it was, he was going to give her a heartache, but how much worse it would be if she spent more time with him? He could shatter her heart into a million pieces.

She traced her fingers across his broad chest, feeling the regular strong beat of his heart, tangling her fingers lightly in his chest hair. "Nick," she whispered, wondering how long it would take her to forget him. How long would it take her to get over him?

How could she ever forget this weekend? Nick was the first in her life. The first man she had given herself to completely in making love.

She wouldn't have regrets there. He had been a consummate lover—sexy, considerate, passionate, unforgettable.

And for that, he would forever be in her memory. She had only herself to blame. She could have said no or resisted him or waited.

Yet she suspected she and Nick would have little time together in the future. She had a bad feeling about what the future held for them.

"Nick," she whispered. At least at this point, she hoped she wasn't wildly in love. She couldn't possibly be because she hadn't known him long enough to be in love.

A tiny voice taunted her about the first encounter she'd had with Nick and how she had floated into the restaurant and wondered if they would ever see each other again. At that moment, she thought he was the most handsome, sexiest man she had ever encountered and she had hoped someday they would get together again and she would get to out with him.

"You're not sleeping," he said quietly. He hadn't moved, but his eyes were open and he was watching her. He surprised her.

"No. I'm watching you sleep."

"That means you can't sleep. What're you thinking about?"

"Remembering that first meeting we had when I tried to keep you from running over the dog."

"I was determined to find you in the restaurant and ask you to go out with me again."

"So here we are."

"I think you're worrying about something and that's why you haven't gone to sleep. You should be relaxed. So whatever's on your mind and creating worries for you—maybe we can do something about that."

"Nick, we've loved for hours."

"Not nearly as much as I want to," he said as he kissed her

throat and made her heartbeat quicken. "See what your pulse does when I kiss you?"

She turned to kiss him and their conversation ended.

It was another hour before she finally did fall asleep in his arms.

The next time she opened her eyes, sunlight poured into the stateroom and Nick was nowhere around.

She showered, dressed in faded cutoffs, a blouse that tied above her bare midriff and sneakers. She found Nick lounging on deck with a steaming pot of coffee, almond biscotti and bright red strawberries. He stood, his gaze drifting over her as he came to meet her. He wrapped her in his arms and smiled. "Good morning," he said, desire twinkling in the depths of his dark brown eyes.

"Good morning," she said, her mouth going dry as want enveloped her and she forgot about the enticing smell of coffee and the delicious fruit. She gazed up at him, needing him as if they hadn't made love yesterday and all through the night.

"Nick," she murmured and stood on tiptoe to wrap her arms around his neck.

He leaned down and his mouth covered hers while his arms tightened around her.

When he released her, he smiled at her. "Come have breakfast."

As she chewed biscotti and sipped her coffee, Nick glanced at his watch. "We'll have to start back." He leaned close and took her hand, rubbing his thumb across her knuckles. "I'll tell you what—why don't we push our conversation about business to dinner tonight. I'll pick you up at seven."

"I have to go see Granddad."

"Go see him. You'll have time to see him and still have dinner with me."

His voice was hoarse, his fingers warm and stirring emotions in her. He leaned close and she looked at his mouth. She nodded. "Yes, I'll go to dinner with you," she said breathlessly, feeling giddy and eager to continue being with him. She knew the time was narrowing until they would be on opposite sides of a big issue. After that was settled, the ill will might be insurmountable.

"All right. Let's have one more swim, a few minutes on the beach and then we'll head home."

She glanced around. "I wondered how much this place influenced us," she said. "You have a movie setting here with the palms, the isolated cove that we have completely to ourselves, the sparkling blue water—it's paradise. Plus your beautiful yacht all to ourselves. Maybe it's all this that seems magical and removed from everyday problems and our world at home."

"It wouldn't have mattered if we'd been in a dark cave that smelled dank. I would have wanted you just as much," he said softly, drawing his fingers across her nape and stirring her.

"I think it would have made a difference. This is enchanted," she said, looking around, memorizing details, yet knowing what would be with her forever were images and memories of Nick. "We're away from our regular lives. It matters, Nick."

"So you'd rather change it?" he asked, his dark eyes watching her closely.

She shook her head. "No. It's just an observation. You're able to compartmentalize your life more easily, I think."

He brushed kisses along her shoulder and then to her ear. "All I know is that I'm with a gorgeous, desirable woman." He raised his head to look intently at her. "I want you more than I did early today. That isn't the way it's supposed to work. You're the one weaving a spell of enchantment, not a bunch of palm fronds, sand and water."

He sounded almost gruff and had a solemn expression that made her heart pound while his words sent her spirits soaring.

"I'm glad it works that way and that I have some effect on you that might be stronger than mere lust."

His eyes narrowed a fraction. "I haven't changed, Julia."

"I know you haven't. Tigers never change their stripes, but it's nice to think when we get home, you aren't going to forget me by this time tomorrow."

His mouth curved in a lazy, crooked grin. "What you're doing to me, I couldn't forget, ever," he said softly, cupping her breast and leaning down to kiss her and start another giddy spiral of love-making. Yet his words spun in her mind and she was thrilled by them.

Was she already falling deeply in love with him? Could she admit the truth to herself? As she kissed him and wound her fingers in his thick hair and ran her other hand over his lean, muscular body, she dismissed her questions as swiftly as they came. She gave herself completely to kissing Nick, wanting to make him hers, wanting him to remember and desire her and melt from her kisses.

She leaned away and framed his face with her hands. "Have you ever really been in love, Nick?"

"Of course, I have," he said, twisting to kiss her fingers while he caressed her breast.

He turned to kiss her again and she forgot questions as she kissed and caressed him.

When they started home, it was later in the day than he had told her. As they sailed out of the cove, she watched the receding beach, wondering if she had lost her heart there along with her virginity.

She turned to look at Nick, who stood at the wheel. She went in to join him, coming up behind him and drinking in the sight of his broad, bare shoulders, narrow hips, long legs, knowing exactly how he felt and tasted and looked beneath the cutoffs he wore.

She wanted to slide her arms around his waist and hug him, but she could feel subtle changes already in both of them. They were heading home, back to real life. They'd had a brief idyll that had been a dream come true, but Nick's heart was already given to driving ambition. What she wanted in the man she loved was permanency, love, devotion. A man who put family first and Nick never would.

She felt a pang, knowing she would continue to see him for a time because she couldn't resist him. She hoped she wasn't really in love with him, that she had been wrapped in a dream world because of the time and place.

Silently, she left the pilothouse and walked to the rail to watch as they rounded a bend and moved out into open water. A wind had sprung up, and there was a chop that was rougher than the sea had been on Friday.

"We're in for a bit of rough riding. Nothing too bad," he said. "There are life jackets here in that locker if you want to wear one."

She nodded and went to put one on. "And you never wear one, do you?"

"Of course, I do. Not right now, but I've been in some big storms. I lost one boat."

"So that reckless streak your younger brother had runs in the family."

Nick grinned and shrugged, turning his attention back to steering. She went outside, standing in the bow riding the rough waves.

They would rise and slap back down. Cool spray blew over her. She looked at the whitecaps and gulls swooping over the water. When she joined Nick again, he reached out to snag her around the waist, pulling her close to kiss her.

She held him tightly, feeling as if he were slipping away from her, having a premonition of disaster waiting at home. Finally, she pushed lightly against his chest and he released her.

"I could drop anchor again," he said in a low voice, placing his hand against her nape.

She shook her head. "We should get home," she said softly and left, knowing she should put distance between them now.

When they stepped back on the dock, Nick carried her briefcase and strode ashore with her, going with her to her parked car. He set her briefcase in her car and then turned to place his hands on her shoulders.

"See you at seven," he said, tracing his forefinger along her chin. "The weekend has been unforgettable—something I never expected," he said in a tone of voice that sounded as if something puzzled him.

"I agree. This week will be something entirely different, Nick."

"Maybe. We can discuss it tonight if you want."

She nodded and slid behind the wheel. "Thanks for the weekend," she said lightly and he leaned down to brush a kiss on her lips.

She drove away without looking back, knowing she would be with Nick again in just hours.

Seven

At six Julia swung open the door and looked up into Nick's dark eyes. Longing for him took her breath away. In a navy suit, a snowy shirt and a navy tie, he was handsome.

His gaze took her in, drifting languidly over her and setting her on fire. He stepped inside to take her into his arms and kiss her while he kicked the door closed behind him. He leaned back against it, pulling her tightly against him.

He was hard, handsome, irresistible. She wanted him with a desperation that shook her. It was as if they had loved and then been separated a year instead of hours. And he had the same hunger. He startled her with his shaking hands as he ran them in her hair that was looped and pinned on her head. Pins flew and she didn't care. She shoved away his coat.

"I want you, Julia!" he rasped. "All I've been able to think about is being with you!" His words increased her eagerness. His hands fluttered over her shoulders and bare back until he found her zipper at her waist. He slid it down while he kissed her and pushed away her sleeveless black silk dress. It fell in a whisper and cool air spilled over her, but she was too hot to notice.

Groaning, Nick leaned back to look at her. She wasn't wearing a bra and his chest expanded when he inhaled. His tan hands cupped her breasts lightly while his thumbs played over her nipples and she gasped with pleasure. As she twisted free the small buttons of his shirt and pushed the starched, cotton shirt off, her hands were as fluttery as his. She unbuckled his belt, unfastening the button at his waist, pulling down the zipper to push away his trousers.

"I couldn't wait to see you," he said. He leaned down to take her breast in his mouth and kiss her. "Beautiful."

"Bedroom?" he queried and she pointed.

They walked backward, a meandering walk with her directing him breathlessly between kisses while clothes were strewn along the way. His briefs and socks were tossed aside; her panty hose and her black thong lay in a heap.

They never reached her bed. Nick leaned against the bedroom wall, picked her up and she locked her long, bare legs around him, sliding down on his throbbing, rock-hard shaft.

With abandon they made love and then sank to the floor exhausted while Nick wrapped her in his tight embrace. He tangled his legs with hers and held her close.

"I'll feed you tonight. We'll dress and go back to plan one."

She laughed against his throat while her fingers skimmed across his smooth jaw. "I think I'll shower first."

"Give me a minute. My legs won't work right now," he said.

Soon they showered together and dressed, and by nine o'clock, they were locked in each other's arms on the dance floor at Nick's petroleum club high above the city on the top floor of the tallest building.

They hardly touched their salmon dinners. They danced to slow numbers wrapped in each other's embrace, barely moving, merely swaying to the music. Her hand was enclosed in his, held against his heart and she had her arm around his neck. She snuggled close, relishing the warmth of his body, pushing aside all warnings that she was involving herself more and more with a man who didn't view life in the manner she did.

By ten, Nick leaned back to look at her. "Want to see my house?"

"Yes," she answered, knowing he implied more than he asked. If they went to his house, they would make love again, maybe through the night, but she knew tomorrow would come too soon.

She also knew that neither one would change the other, not on business, not on lifestyles—the real unbridgeable chasm, even if they settled their business differences amicably.

They passed her house on their way to his and in a few blocks turned to wait while tall, black iron gates swung open. Nick drove up a wide, winding drive to a tall Georgian mansion with a fountain in front of the porch that was graced with half a dozen mammoth Corinthian columns.

Nick circled the house, parking in front of the eight-car garage.

She didn't see any more of his house than she guessed he had of hers because they moment they stepped inside the entryway at the back, they were in each other's arms and made it no farther than the thick carpet in front of a fireplace in the kitchen.

Later, Nick carried her to bed and she spent most of the night in his arms, but by four in the morning, she slipped out of bed to gather her clothes.

"I can take you home anytime. Come back to bed," Nick said in a seductive voice that slithered hotly her. He lay sprawled on his side, long and powerful, and she was tempted to go flying back to him. His chest hair was a dark mat in contrast to the creamy satin sheet that lay in folds across his hips and long legs. Locks of his dark hair fell over his forehead, adding to his appeal. It was pure temptation to do what he asked.

Taking a deep breath and reminding herself what she should do, she shook her head. "No. For once I'm going to resist your charms. I have to go home, Nick."

He swung out of bed and she inhaled. He was aroused, sexy, naked.

She turned away swiftly and stepped into her dress pulling it up.

When she reached for the zipper, he already had it in his fingers and he leaned down to shower kisses across her back as he tugged up the zipper. As he caressed her, she glanced over her shoulder at him.

"We have to go," she whispered, wondering if he had any idea how difficult he was making it for her to leave. He pulled on clothes while she finished dressing.

"Want a tour of my house before you go?" he asked. She glanced beyond him at the enormous master bedroom that was a suite. He had a king-size four-poster that looked over two hundred years old. Both a tall dresser and an ornately carved armoire matched the bed and a gilt floor-to-ceiling mirror was across from the bed.

"You surprise me with your beautiful antiques, Nick."

"Why the surprise? I like beautiful things," he stated in a velvet tone while he caressed her nape.

"You just don't seem the type to give much time or attention to your surroundings." She turned away, crossing the polished oak floor and heading for the hall.

"I give a lot of attention to my surroundings." Nick caught up with her and held her arm as they walked down a sweeping staircase that curved to an entrance hall below. "We can take a quick tour. I want you to see my house. I want to know you, and I want you to know me," he added.

"I should go," she said, glancing through double doors into a formal room that had Corinthian columns, oriental rugs and gilt-framed oil paintings on the walls. "And you do have a beautiful home."

"Thank you. This house is the formal one. My ranch house is casual. So is the villa at Cozumel and the cabin in the Rockies. I hope I get to show you all of them," he said and her pulse quickened at all he implied. At the same time, she reminded herself that they really didn't have a future together.

He slipped his arm around her waist and they walked to the

back door where he readied the alarm before he locked the door behind them.

They waited for the gates at the end of his drive to swing open. She rode in silence, knowing every tick of the clock was taking them closer to saying goodbye forever.

He drove the short distance to pull up in her driveway where he got out to accompany her to her door. They stood on her wraparound porch while he brushed her hair away from her face. "It's been another fabulous night."

"We'll see each other in a few hours."

"You don't mind that we never discussed business?"

"What good would it have done either one of us?" she asked with amusement.

"I can listen and change sometimes. If there is a good reason."

"I rather doubt your answer. And I'm sure it doesn't apply in this situation."

"Four days until we all meet. That means you and I can continue to go without a storm between us for the next few days. So let me pick you up tomorrow night."

"We can eat here," she said.

He smiled and nodded. "And since I can't wait until evening to see you, meet me for lunch. Where will you be around noon?"

She laughed. "Nick, you're impossible. I have a ten o'clock appointment at State Bank, the branch on Highland."

"Meet me at Gregory's Café at half-past eleven. That will give you time, won't it? You can call me if you're earlier or later. I'll be there." He leaned down and brushed a kiss on her cheek before he turned to walk to his car. She watched his long-legged purposeful stride, wondering if Thursday night he would walk right out of her life forever.

She gave a small shake of her shoulders and stepped inside, turning off the alarm and locking up, and then setting the alarm again before she went to her bedroom. As she walked through her house, she looked at the polished oak floors, the oil paintings she owned, her formal living room that was furnished in cherrywood and a pale blue decor. Her home was attractive, livable. His was magnificent and a museum. Hers was kid-friendly and his was not, but then Nick didn't intend to have any kids running through his house. Four more days of Nick. How long would it take to get over him?

She set the alarm, knowing if she could catch even thirty minutes of sleep she would feel more refreshed and ready for the day. They had this week until Friday to make a last-ditch effort to save the company; for her grandfather's sake, she would try as hard as she could to thwart Nick.

She imagined the dealings Friday would cause a split with Nick, but it was a split that was inevitable; business just moved up the timetable slightly. Nick was blind with ambition, chasing success, and not the man for her. If only her heart could get the message!

She had an appointment at ten with Leon Jefferson, a banker her grandfather had known for years. Because the vice president was running late with another appointment, the receptionist asked her to wait with an apology, so Julia sat in a tan wingback chair in the lobby and picked up a magazine. While customers moved around her, she turned pages until she was startled to hear a familiar voice.

She recognized the voice of Tyler Wade, Nick's vice president, and turned in her chair to say hello. When she saw him greet a friend of his, she didn't speak. Wanting to avoid interrupting the two men, she settled in her chair and planned to say hello to Tyler when he finished his conversation. As she glanced through the magazine, Tyler's mention of Nick caught her attention, and she couldn't resist listening.

"You've got to come out and see this yearling," Tyler said.

"I thought that damn sorrel was Nick Ransome's prize. I've offered him a small fortune to buy it."

Tyler laughed. "I proposed something better. I thought I might have a chance to win his colt if he made a bet with me."

"What the hell did Nick bet with you and lose?"

"I bet him I could name a woman he couldn't seduce within two weeks." Julia stiffened and chilled, unable now to stop listening to Tyler.

"Yeah, I'll bet she was over ninety," the stranger scoffed.

Tyler chuckled. "Nope. Just beautiful, single, under thirty, a knockout, unattached and a woman of my choice."

"Sounds like Nick Ransome's type. What did you stand to lose?"

"My Ferrari," Tyler replied, and Julia wondered who the woman was that Tyler was talking about.

"I can't imagine that either one of you would take a bet like that."

"I really thought I had a chance. The lady doesn't like Nick. They're business rivals," he said, and another icy jolt hit Julia. She listened as Tyler continued. "I chose a woman who could resist him and collected royally. He tried to seduce her for revenge over business deals and took her sailing for the weekend. But surprise, surprise—the lady withstood Nick's charms. I should take her out for a steak dinner at Fort Worth's best. Anyway, come watch Standing Tall."

"I will. Maybe I can name a price that you'd take for the colt."

"Not in a million years. This horse is going to be a winner and Nick knew it, too. Come to my place eleven Saturday morning and we'll go to lunch after you've seen my horses."

"Great, Tyler. I'll see you Saturday."

"Miss Holcomb," the smiling receptionist said as she approached Julia, "please come with me." No longer caring to be seen by Tyler, she followed the receptionist to a corner office, and as she shook hands with Leon Jefferson, she couldn't get her thoughts off Nick and his bet.

In spite of the working relationship between her grandfather and the banker, Leon Jefferson politely turned down her request for an extension on their loan.

Her grandfather had gotten too extended, too bogged down in loans and exploration, and was now vulnerable, especially to Nick.

Numb, Julia stepped into the sunshine following her meeting and crossed the expanse of paving, not noticing the immaculate flowerbeds filled with bright yellow marigolds and red and white periwinkles.

Worry nagged at her, but along with it her fury was hot and thick. She was supposed to have lunch with Nick. She could cancel by phone or just stand him up.

Anger rocked her and she debated whether to go to the office or just go home to be alone and cool down.

She opted for the office, where hopefully she could get her mind off Nick. She turned her sports car onto a boulevard, moving into a stream of traffic.

Nick had told Tyler he had lost the bet, but that didn't matter. Seduction had been revenge for him. Waves of anger buffeted her, and she forced herself to concentrate on her driving.

In minutes, she pulled into the tree-shaded office parking lot and climbed out to hurry to her large, corner office on the tenth floor. She told her brunette secretary, Angela, that she didn't want to be disturbed and she wasn't taking phone calls for the next hour. Let Nick cool his heels at the restaurant; she didn't care.

She closed the door to her office and glanced around at familiar surroundings that usually gave her a sense of satisfaction. Green plants, oil paintings, a floor with a thick beige carpet and comfortable leather furniture filled the room. Near floor-to-ceiling windows was a large ebony table that she used for a desk. She had an adjoining bathroom, small sitting room, closet and a tiny wet bar in a corner of her office.

She walked to the closet to toss her purse inside a built-in drawer. She shed the jacket to her suit and then walked to the window to look outside. From the tenth floor she had a good view of the city. Nick was out there, waiting at a restaurant for her. At the thought of him, her cell phone rang. She ignored it.

Seduction for revenge and she had succumbed eagerly! She clung to fury because her anger covered her hurt.

After ten minutes and two more calls on her cell, she moved away from the window. She had to forget Nick. Do something that would take her mind off him. She could see no way of stopping him from acquiring Holcomb, but she pulled out the books to look at figures to see if she could think of any possibilities. She withdrew a ledger of possible places they could get more financing, knowing this had been gone over and over long ago.

As she looked at the books, her thoughts still spun around Nick. She couldn't get him out of mind and that added to her anger.

A commotion in the reception room caught her attention and she saw her secretary standing, arguing with someone and waving her hands. Then Angela walked around her desk, heading toward Julia's door and Julia lost sight of her. She could guess who was arguing with Angela and she moved around in front of her desk, wondering if Angela could manage to keep Nick out.

The door swung open and Angela tried to pass Nick, thrusting her head around him. "I'm sorry. He insisted—"

"That's all right, Angela. You can close the door please," Julia said, barely aware of what she'd told her secretary. Her gaze was locked with Nick's.

In spite of her anger, the moment she spotted him in his navy suit and tie, her pulse raced. Too often her desire was tangled with her anger where Nick was concerned. As he approached her, his eyes narrowed.

"Something's wrong," he said quietly stopping within inches of her and placing on hand on her shoulder. "Why didn't you show up for lunch or call me? You aren't taking your calls. What's happened?"

She felt as if his probing brown eyes were going straight through her and that he knew her every thought. Her anger boiled over again. "I saw Tyler at the bank, but he didn't see me."

"And?" Nick asked, sounding puzzled.

"And I overheard him talking about you wanting revenge."

Nick grimaced, his eyes now flashing with fire. "Dammit! Julia—"

"My seduction was a bet with Tyler to get revenge on my family in just one more way," she said, keeping her voice down, but unable to bank the fury rocking her.

Taking her arm, Nick inhaled. "Damn Tyler anyway! I told him that I lost the bet."

"That hardly matters. What matters is that you took me with you for a weekend to seduce me with cold calculation and get some more revenge for old hurts. That's the lowest—"

"Listen to me," Nick ordered in a firm voice, squeezing her shoulder lightly. "I was angry with your grandfather and wanted revenge. I'll admit it. I still think if they find the culprit that sabotaged our rig, there will be a connection to Holcomb."

"If there is, Granddad knows nothing about it," she said and Nick shrugged.

"I was angry and wanted revenge and made the damn bet with Tyler. After spending time with you, revenge and anger toward you went out of mind."

"You're a very smooth talker, Nick. You know how to manipulate and charm people and get what you want. But this bet tramples all over my trust." She looked into his brown eyes that gazed unwaveringly at her and she wondered how much she could ever trust him from here on. She would never know the truth about his declaration because it was all past and done now.

"Do you think I would have told Tyler I lost my bet and give up my prize horse if I still wanted revenge? Do you, Julia?" Nick insisted.

She sighed and shook her head and felt some of her anger with him subside. "I suppose not."

"Hardly. Tyler is ecstatic to get my horse. I could have had his Ferarri and kept my damn horse. He's filled with glee because he thinks I struck out with you. Does that sound as if I'm lying to you about the bet?"

"No, it doesn't," she admitted. She stared at him, wishing they could settle all the differences between them as easily. "There's a ruthless streak in you, Nick, to make the bet in the first place and try and get revenge in seduction that is so tied with someone's—in this case, my—emotions."

"All right. I shouldn't have even toyed with the idea, but I dropped it totally. I told you that I was angry and made the bet in the heat of anger. Just keep that in mind. When we made love, there was not one degree of revenge in my thought. I wanted you, Julia," he said hoarsely, sliding his hand to her nape. "I wanted you more than I've ever wanted a woman in my life."

She ached to believe him, but she couldn't believe the last statement. She couldn't imagine evoking such desire in a man like Nick.

"Nick!" she exclaimed in an exasperated sigh. "What can I believe? You're a charmer and you weave spells. Your reason for the past weekend was—"

"I told you. I tossed that aside before we made love. Forget it, Julia. It had nothing to do with what took place between us. I swear I'm telling you the truth."

His voice was earnest, his expression solemn and desire burned as hotly in his brown eyes as ever. Despite her anger and their arguments and opposing goals, he took her breath away and she wanted him right now, with more urgent desperation than ever.

Something flickered in the depths of his eyes and he inhaled, his chest expanding with his breath. He slid his arm around her waist and her heart raced. "I wanted you when we were out there. I wanted you with all my being more than I've ever wanted anyone. That's the damn truth, Julia."

His words burned her anger to cinders. He was believable, totally convincing. Dazed, she looked up at him and trembled from her toes to her head. "You can always tell what I'm thinking."

"See? We're in sync sometimes." He pulled her to him and leaned down to kiss her, a hard, possessive kiss that made her forget her surroundings, her arguments, her hurt and anger. His kiss was a brand and a declaration that left no doubt that he wanted her. His lips moved on hers and his tongue thrust deep, awakening every nerve. He groaned and leaned over her and she arched against him eagerly. This kiss was different, more intense, as if his kiss would convince that his words were true.

And it made her feel wanted by him totally, urgently enough to turn her knees to mush and build her desire to a raging fire.

"Nick," she whispered, trying to think and regain some control. "We're in my office. We're not—"

"Where can we go?" he murmured, looking around. He dropped his arm around her waist and pulled her into her sitting room, shutting the door. Windows spilled sunshine from the outside, but otherwise they were closed off. He pulled her into his embrace and leaned over her, kissing her as possessively as before.

"I want you more than you can ever know," he said softly and then his mouth came down on hers again.

She wound her fingers in his hair, kissing him back with the same fiery passion, letting her desire for him run rampant.

With shaking hands, he peeled her out of her tailored suit skirt and panty hose while she unfastened his belt and freed him from his slacks.

"You're crazy, Nick," she sighed, wanting him, knowing they were in her office and should wait. His words and kisses had set her on fire. How could she resist or wait when he made her feel as if he had to have her to survive?

Standing on tiptoe and wrapping her arms around his neck, she responded, kissing him passionately. He moved to lean back against a wall and picked her up. She wrapped her legs around him while she kissed him and he slid her down on his hard shaft.

He groaned, kissing her with the same urgent fervor as before. Desire consumed her. She moved her hips with him, hearing him call her name dimly above the roaring of her pulse in her ears.

"Julia, love!" he gasped and his tongue thrust into her mouth.

Frantically she moved with him, seeking release while tension coiled and burned inside her.

Her climax exploded in fury; then his release came, and he pumped fast and hard. Knowing their loving forged another link in a chain binding her heart to him, she held him tightly and wished she never had to let go.

They gasped for breath while they clung to each other.

"Thank heaven, there's a shower in my bathroom. It's small, but it works."

He kissed her throat and gazed into her eyes while he still held her. "I meant everything I said to you. I want you more than I've ever wanted anyone."

Her heart skipped a beat and she thrilled at his words, even though she knew they were headed for calamity no matter what each of them wanted.

"We have such differences, Nick. Sooner or later, they're going to matter."

"Just take today," he said in a gruff voice. "Let's not worry about the future."

She slid her legs down him and stood, but he didn't release her. Brown curls clung damply to his forehead and she pushed them back while she shook her head. "Nick, this is outrageous! We're in my office and I should go shower and dress."

"Let me just hold you a minute," he whispered and she couldn't refuse. Her arms were under his white cotton shirt, locked around his waist.

"Julia, we can weather the business deal. You told me all that matters is your grandfather and in the long run, he's going to be better off and have fewer worries."

"We'll see. You just told me to take one day at a time."

"So I did and I will. This day is turning out to be a fine one." Nick raked his fingers through her hair slowly. "Julia, I lost my prize racehorse to Tyler. You should have an inkling of what that horse means to me. It was Standing Tall, my best horse and one I had great expectations pinned on. I could have had Tyler's Ferrari if I'd wanted. Instead, he has my dream horse."

Startled, she stared at him. "Standing Tall? Your best horse?" The implications of what Nick had been telling her began to sink in. "You did that?"

"Yes, I did."

His sacrifice stunned her. As badly as Nick liked to win, how could he have given away his best horse when he actually won the bet? She took a deep breath and wondered how deep Nick's feelings really ran for her.

"I need to get on some clothes," she said, trying to remember they should dress.

"We'll shower together," he said, scooping her into his arms. She pointed toward the bathroom and Nick set her down in the narrow shower stall.

"I'm not sure this together is a good idea, Nick, and I want to keep my hair dry."

"It's a fabulous idea. Afterwards, we'll go to lunch," he said as he turned on a spray of warm water and began to lightly soap her with his hands, running them slowly over her breasts.

She inhaled with pleasure and closed her eyes, catching his wrists. "Nick, stop. I have an appointment at two and I want that lunch before then."

"All right if you'll promise to let me do this tonight," he said softly, kissing her neck and sliding his hand down over her bottom.

"I promise," she breathed, her thoughts still mulling over Nick giving up his horse. She would never have figured he'd do such a thing and it made her wonder about him. "We're getting bound more and more together with chains that are going to hurt when they break. But then you never have known heartbreak."

"Have you?" he asked.

"No, and I don't want to now," she replied.

"Back to one day at a time, remember?"

"For now, but pretty soon, Nick, we have to talk about what we each want."

"That's incredibly easy. What I want is you, delicious," he murmured, kissing the corner of her mouth, "beautiful," he added, kissing her breast, "soft and curvy and exciting."

His words wove a spell of magic. "Stop your seduction," she murmured. "I have to work today and we're not making love again in my little shower."

"Nope, but you promised tonight…" His voice faded away. She soaped him, unable to resist and in minutes they both kissed passionately while water poured over them.

She wriggled away and stepped out of the shower. "That's it, Nick. I'm getting ready for lunch."

They dressed swiftly and when she left her office, Julia felt her cheeks flush as Angela looked back and forth between them. "I'm sure you met Nick Ransome," Julia said.

Angela reached out to shake hands with him. "I've heard so much about you," she said. "I'm glad to meet you."

"I hope what you heard was good," Nick said lightly, glancing at Julia before taking Angela's hand and shaking it briefly. "It's nice to meet you."

"I'll be gone until four," Julia said. "I'm going to lunch and then I have a two o'clock appointment. I have my cell phone."

Her secretary nodded and looked back at Nick, smiling at him.

As Julia walked down the hall with him, she said. "I'm sure she realizes you may be her new employer starting Friday, so I doubt if she put up much fight to keep you out of my office."

"I was so busy thinking about seeing you, I didn't notice," Nick said. He punched the button for the elevator and turned to look at Julia. There was speculation in his gaze and she wondered what was running through his mind.

They had the elevator to themselves and Nick pulled her into his arms for a quick kiss. As they stopped and the doors opened, he took her arm. "There aren't nearly enough floors in this building."

"You do just as you please. I can't believe we made love in the middle of the day in my office. That's as public as this lobby."

"No, it wasn't. Might be sometimes, but it wasn't today. We had it to ourselves."

"Angela had to know what we were doing," she replied.

"Doesn't matter. I could happily kiss you right here and now."

"Don't you think about it!" she snapped, and he grinned and shrugged.

"Why not? I want you to be my woman."

"'My woman?' That sounds like something out of the Dark Ages," she protested.

"Not at all."

She stopped and tilted her head and looked up at him. "Nick Ransome, is this a proposal?"

He grinned and shook his head. "Not the kind you have in mind." His smile faded and he studied her solemnly. "Julia, I'm asking you to move into my house. Have you thought of that possibility? We could make love all we want when we want. We could hold each other through the night every night."

"You know that's not what I want."

"You act like you might want it," he said.

She was aware they stood in the busy lobby of her office building. People walked past them without a glance. "Why are we into this very private conversation now?"

"Because it came up and it's important. What do you want, Julia?"

"You know what I want. I told you when we were on your yacht. I want it all, the ring, the permanency, the babies, lifelong commitment."

"I can't do that and I think I made that clear before."

"You did, so there's no future for us."

"But there's today. Stay at my house tonight. Come over and I'll cook and you stay and let me love you all night and hold you close for hours." His voice lowered and became silky and ran over her like a caress.

What temptation he flung at her! She wanted to say yes to whatever she could have of him. If she were with him constantly, he might fall in love with her later. She stopped that train of thought that could delude her and lead to more trouble than she already had.

"C'mon. Agree with me," he coaxed. "You want to. I can see it in your expression and we'll have a fabulous night. Say, yes, Julia," he said, stroking her cheek.

"Yes, tonight, but there will come a tomorrow."

"You're right, of course, but for now I can look forward with anticipation for tonight and I don't have to think about the future."

"Someday, Nick, you're going to get in too deep to get out and you'll wonder what you've done to yourself," she said. She wanted to kiss him—hot, passionately—make him think of her the rest of the day and be anxious to be with her. But she was in her company's lobby with familiar people passing them. This wasn't the time or place.

They went to lunch and parted with Julia agreeing to be at his house at seven. She worked through most of the afternoon, keeping appointments she had made before she knew Nick, trying to get Holcomb solvent and knowing it was impossible.

Discouraged, hoping tomorrow would bring some kind of response, she talked briefly to her grandfather and to company accountants. Then she left for home. With every turn of the tires taking her closer to her house, her excitement grew. She would be with Nick tonight and he had a point about taking things one day at a time. In bubbling eagerness, she dressed in emerald slacks and an emerald shirt.

When she drove up Nick's drive, he was standing outside. At the sight of him, her pulse leaped. Dressed in tight jeans and a T-shirt that clung to his sculpted muscles, he motioned her to the back. When she stepped out of the car, he strolled up.

Nick enveloped her in his embrace. "I've been waiting forever," he said in a husky voice.

"Liar!" she accused, knowing Nick did not stand around and wait for anything.

He ended the conversation as he kissed her. "Now my evening begins," he said when he leaned back to look down at her. "Come in and see my house."

It was hours later before he gave her a tour of his house, and they ate dinner after ten that night. She sat in a kitchen alcove, looking out at a dazzling blue swimming pool that had a sparkling fountain in the center.

They had both showered and dressed and she gazed outside at the patio with its baskets of colorful flowers. Nick sipped a glass of water, ice cubes clinking slightly as he set the glass back on the table.

"Wednesday night Matt wants to have us out to his ranch for dinner. My dad will be there and my sister is coming in. The whole family tries as much as we can to get together at least once a month."

"So, you're close with your family?"

"Yes. We've tried to do this since we got out of college, but there are times some of us are away. We bring friends, too. It's casual." He gave her a long level look, and she wondered what was on his mind. She waited in silence. "Will you go with me Wednesday night?" he asked finally. "I'd like you to meet my family. I like to have you with me as much as I can, so why not take you to our family gathering? I'll enjoy the evening more if you're there."

Her heart swelled with his declaration of wanting her with him. She stared at him and wondered if he really wanted to have her with him. "I'd be delighted to go," she said carefully, and he smiled.

"You sound as if I asked you to eat in a burning house."

She laughed in return and shook her head. "No, you just surprised me."

"Don't worry, my family is just getting together for dinner and I want you with me whether we're with my family or somewhere else. Besides, we've always brought friends with us."

Julia nodded, but as they ate and she listened to Nick talk, she wondered about the approaching family dinner. He made it sound casual and as if the Ransomes invited outsiders regularly, but a family dinner meant she was getting to know Nick and those close to him. And he wanted her with him as much as possible—how deep did that go?

She felt as if she were sinking into an abyss where she couldn't escape with her heart intact. The family dinner might mean nothing to Nick or any of his siblings and father, but it meant a lot to her. She would know his family, know him better, be closer to all of them, be more familiar with the Ransome homes and lives. It was definitely moving her into their inner circle and she knew it wasn't wise on her part. But as always, Nick was impossible to resist.

Wednesday night, her curiosity grew with each mile as they sped through the Texas country, leaving the city for the wide-open spaces. As they raced along a highway that had little traffic, she watched Nick drive. Nick's strong hands moved on the wheel, but all she could recall was his hands moving over her. His fingers were well-shaped, the nails blunt. He was in slacks and a Polo, and she wore her yellow slacks and yellow silk shirt. She wanted to reach over and touch him, but he was concentrating on his driving and she left him alone.

She thought about their time together. Only one more day stood between them and a showdown over the Holcomb company.

After Friday morning, Julia wondered if she would see Nick again. She suspected she would not, but life was filled with un-expected twists and turns.

As Nick raced over the cattle guard, she knew she was the first member of her family to ever set foot on the Ransome ranch.

"Stop looking worried. My family is friendly. Matt and his wife have a baby, little Jeff. Dad has mellowed. Katherine is too busy to notice much of anything."

"You see too much. Most people can't guess whether I'm worried or sad or happy if I don't want them to," Julia answered.

"First of all, you don't have to hide your feelings from me, and second of all, I can tell by looking at you."

"Scary," she teased, but she wondered about his answer. And then it was forgotten.

When they pulled up to a sprawling ranch house, her trepi-dation increased. She was reluctant to meet his family. They didn't know each other that well, and generations of hate had existed between the men in their two families. As Nick slammed the car door and came around the car to open her door, she wished she could skip this night.

He held open the door and she stepped outside. Nick slipped his arm around her waist. "Come meet everyone," he said.

Eight

They crossed a green lawn that had a profusion of flowers in well-tended beds. On the porch, the hanging pots of yellow bougainvillea, scarlet gaillardia and purple impatiens couldn't cheer Julia.

When they entered the house through the kitchen, Julia met his family. His brother Matt bore a family resemblance; he shook her hand warmly while he kept his arm around the shoulders of his wife. Holding a sleeping baby, Olivia Ransome flashed a warm smile and greeted Julia. Katherine Ransome was equally welcoming, studying Julia with the same intentness that Nick sometimes did.

It was Duke Ransome, whose blue eyes were glacial, who stared at her as if she were in an enemy camp. His handshake was perfunctory, and she suspected he didn't approve of his son seeing her or of her being included in a family dinner.

"How's your grandfather?" Duke asked.

"He's fine," she replied, and Duke nodded, turning to talk to Nick. It was the last time Duke gave her any attention or talked to her. Later in the evening. when she was alone in the kitchen with Katherine, Nick's sister stepped close.

"Don't worry about Dad. When he meets people, he's cold at first."

"I'll bet not all people. I know we go way back with lots of animosity between our families, so I'm not surprised."

Katherine leaned against the kitchen counter, her crystal blue eyes sparkling as she studied Julia. "Can I ask you a question?"

"Sure, go ahead," Julia responded, wondering what Katherine had in mind that she felt she needed permission to ask.

"Are you serious about Nick?"

Startled, Julia stared at her and shook her head. "No," she said, turning away before she revealed more than she wanted it to. Katherine might have the same keen perception about people that her older brother did.

"I think Nick's serious about you," Katherine said in a quiet voice, and Julia turned around to stare at her again.

"Oh, I don't think Nick gets serious about any woman. You of all people, should know that."

"He sure hasn't before, but I've seen the way he looks at you. He isn't casual with you. He's intense."

"I don't think it means anything."

"I know my brother. Your relationship with Nick may be more serious than you realize."

Julia shook her head. "No, I can promise you it's not. We have a lot of business differences, but those aren't really important. It's our lifestyles and goals that will always cause a rift between us. Nick is not a marrying man."

"That's exactly what my brother Matt said. Now look at him. Married and loving it. Nick might change his mind, but then again, he might not. You could live with him and take your chances if y'all have a thing going between you."

"No. That life isn't for me. Absolutely not," she said, surprised at how easy it was to talk to Katherine. She felt as if Katherine was her friend, and it seemed as if she had known her for years instead of hours. "I know what I want and I'm not settling for something partial or temporary," Julia said quietly.

Katherine gave her a long look before she pushed away from the counter. "Too bad. Nick hasn't wanted to marry. After the way he grew up, there's not much appeal in it. I hope the business deal works out for you, too. I don't keep up with Nick's work, even when it's the energy company. I've got enough to worry about with my own company and I know Nick will take care of things."

"Yes, he will."

"Well, it's been nice to meet you."

"I don't think your dad wanted to meet me at all."

"That's just Dad. He holds old grudges." Katherine brushed locks of hair out of her eyes.

"Has my sister pinned you to the wall?" Nick asked, sauntering into the room and looking warmly at Julia as he crossed the room to her.

"Uh-oh," Katherine said. "Time to exit," she added and disappeared through the door.

Nick wrapped his hands around Julia's waist. "Having a good time? Katherine probably was Miss Twenty Questions."

"Yes, I am having a fine time. You have an interesting, friendly family."

"Good. I like them and I'm glad you do. If you can tear yourself away, it's time to start home. Ready?"

"Yes, I am," she said. His words *it's time to start home* gave her a thrill and a pang at the same time. It sounded as if they were a married couple; how she wished that were so. She looked up into Nick's dark eyes, letting her gaze drift down to his mouth. She realized in that moment that she was in love with him. Hopelessly lost. After Thursday night, she would move out of his house and get back on her own, but she was in love with him. What would it hurt if she stayed longer?

Just a bigger heartbreak. She knew tomorrow night was the last. Thursday was time to end it. They would disagree on the business deal, so this would be a good time to break away even though the break was caused by something far removed from business.

They told the family goodbye and Julia gave Matt and Olivia her thanks for a wonderful evening and repeated how cute their baby was. Duke Ransome's expression was as cold as it had been early in the evening. Katherine gave Julia a light hug. "Come see us again," she exclaimed.

Nick held Julia's arm and they hurried to the car.

In the dark as he drove back to Dallas, Julia pondered what Katherine had said about Nick being intense.

She watched him drive just as she had earlier. Now lights from the dash splashed over him and highlighted his prominent cheekbones, the long, straight slope of his nose, his sculpted mouth.

"You have a great family."

"Dad's probably a little like your granddad. They're another generation from another time. They're cranky sometimes, stubborn, smart. Wiley old codgers who have survived all these years. Dad sees you as a Holcomb. He's not going to warm up to you instantly."

"If ever," she added dryly. "I don't think he will any more than my grandfather will welcome you into our midst. It's just as well we're not going further, Nick, you and I, because members of both our families wouldn't like it."

"And would that really matter to you?" he asked her.

"Yes, it would. Granddad and I are close. I want the man in my life to get along with Granddad and vice versa."

"I'll admit I used to have animosity toward him and your dad, but it's gone now."

She studied him and wondered if he had really lost the ill will. "Probably because you finally won."

"Probably because of daughter and granddaughter," Nick added dryly. "They're part of you. That makes a difference."

She was surprised that it would make a difference or that she might be that important in Nick's life. What did he feel for her?

"Your sister is very pretty."

"Katie—I guess. She's my sister and that's all I ever see. Kid sister, at that. She had a bum romance and she's a little bitter now."

"Too bad. All of you are a little sour on marriage."

"But not on love," he drawled softly, brushing kisses across her knuckles again. His breath was warm. "I know you have to stay buckled in, but I'd like you in my lap."

"Soon enough, Nick. I'm going home with you."

"Don't say it reluctantly. I think my family visit worried you."

"No, I just think they got all excited because they think you're serious about somebody, and that isn't the case."

"I'm fairly serious."

She had to laugh. "As serious as a tiger about a chunk of meat."

He smiled and this time traced his tongue over her palm. She withdrew her hand. "Wait until we're at your house. You keep your attention on the road."

"Much more inviting to keep it on you. I know this road like my own hand and we're still almost an hour away from our houses and from me getting to make love to you," he said in a low voice that thrilled her.

She couldn't resist and placed her hand on his warm thigh. He immediately covered her hand with his. "I want you home. I want you in my bed. I just want you."

"I don't think your attention is totally on your driving."

"Sure as hell isn't," he said. "We could pull off the road into the bushes."

When she laughed, he glanced at her. "I'm serious."

"Home, please. Maybe we'll even get as far as a bed. I'm going to miss you, Nick. Miss you badly."

"So where are you going? And when?"

"I figure probably tomorrow night is our last night together."

"How in sweet hell do you figure that?"

"Friday, you buy out Holcomb and my grandfather will be in a rage. I'll have to move on. And I would have to eventually anyway."

"Back to long-term commitment, aren't we?"

"Not necessarily," she answered with a lightness she was far from feeling. But she didn't want him to know she had fallen in love with him. She didn't want him to ever know it. When she walked out of his life, she didn't want to give him a guilt trip. And sooner or later, if she didn't walk, he would. Better her, and the sooner the better.

"Nick, you're going to break the sound barrier," she said, glancing at the speedometer.

"This is a straight road that I know absolutely and I can't wait to get you home into my arms so I can kiss you the rest of the night."

She looked out the dark window and anticipation curled in her. She wanted the same thing he did, to make love until morning.

When they reached his house, the minute the door closed behind him, she reached for him. Clothing was strewn across the back entryway through the kitchen and into the hall. Nick turned her into the family room and they made love on the thick carpet.

Later, he held her close and combed her hair from her face. "There are some thirty-six rooms in this house and I want to make love to you in every one of them," he murmured.

"Ridiculous!" she said, laughing.

"I love it when you laugh. I don't want tomorrow night to be our last night. Not that one, Julia."

She looked away from his velvety dark eyes and thought about their future. "I think after tomorrow, you'll feel differently about it."

"You barely have anything here of yours. Wait until tomorrow and let's see how you feel. Until a week ago, none of this would have been an issue. Just wait. Don't do anything."

"Nick, you're prolonging what's inevitable. You and I are on different wavelengths about our futures."

He wrapped his arms around her and pulled her tightly into his embrace, wrapping his long, bare legs with hers.

She ran her fingers over him, down across his washboard belly, his muscled thigh. "Are we going to argue all night?" she asked.

"Sure as hell not," he said, pulling her closer again so he could kiss her.

Through the night, they made love, showered and talked, and every moment held a bittersweet edge because she was certain she was moving closer to saying goodbye.

Thursday passed in a blur and that night she was back in Nick's arms and bed, loving him wildly, savoring each moment.

She was learning more about him and now everything he wanted was tied directly to success in some business endeavor. She tried to make the most of the moment and bank her mounting disappointment. Finally, near dawn, he fell asleep in her arms. She watched him for a long time, looking at his chest rise and fall, the thick mat of hair that covered his chest, his tangled hair that fell over his forehead.

She finally drifted to sleep and woke in his arms to find him watching her. "It's early," she murmured drowsily, glancing at the gray light in the windows. "We don't have to stir yet."

"Then come here," he said, pulling her closer. "I'm sure that we can find something entertaining to do until the sun is fully up."

"Speaking about something being up—" she said playfully, running her hands over him.

She caressed him, moving over him as they began making love again. This time she threw herself into the passion more than ever, shaking with desire, knowing this might be their last time together.

It was another two hours before they showered and dressed. As Nick tied his necktie, he turned to her. "I want to have lunch with you."

"Sorry, I promised Granddad a long time ago. Let's not set plans, Nick."

He shrugged and turned back and she watched him dress for a moment. He was as darkly handsome as ever and she wanted to walk right back into his arms, but she knew she couldn't.

She realized he was watching her in the mirror, staring at her as she dressed. She moved away because they needed to get going. Nick had promised to take her home so she could get her own car.

In another hour, they had dressed and eaten. Nick pulled into her driveway to let her out. "I want to take you to dinner—how's that, instead of lunch?"

"We'll see, Nick, how things go. I'm not promising anything at this point."

He climbed out of the car to walk her to her door. "Remember, this is just business. It has nothing to do with our private lives."

"It does with yours because it's be-all and end-all to you, everything."

"I can compartmentalize it, Julia. I have a private life, a personal life. I can shut off the other."

"I doubt if they've often been in conflict," she answered coolly. "I'll see you with your lawyers at ten, Nick."

"Look," he said, placing his hand over her head on the doorjamb and leaning closer, hemming her in. He ran his other hand back and forth beneath her collar. "I don't want to call it quits. I don't want to stop seeing each other. We set each other on fire. Why give that up?"

"There are other considerations and you know it. That's lust, Nick. I keep telling you—I want it all. I want more than lust and your desire. I want the total, lifetime commitment. We're not even in love," she said, her words sounding hollow.

"Dammit, I'm in love!" he snapped. He pulled her to him and kissed her hard, another demanding, possessive kiss that rocked her and left no doubt that he wanted her desperately. She wound her arms around his neck and kissed him back. Their physical relationship was good and she wondered if she was doing something she would regret forever.

He leaned back. "I want you. You're mine."

She shook her head. "I'm not yours and you're not mine. You know that. Love is union, but it's not possession. I have to go, Nick." She brushed past him and opened her door and stepped inside.

She turned to look at him, finding him watching her intently.

"At least give me a chance and say you'll go to dinner with me tonight," he said. "You can do that much. One more dinner isn't going to do you in."

"Promise to bring me right back here when I'm ready."

"Of course I will," he answered solemnly.

"All right. I'll go with you."

He let out his breath and then raised his head to look at her. "How about seven? Pick you up here."

"Fine. But it might be subject to change."

He ground his jaw closed and stared at her. "I'll see you soon."

She closed the door and sagged against it. Her lips tingled from his kiss and she burned with desire. She could never get enough of him!

At the sound of his car driving away, she opened her eyes and went to her room to change clothes. She just hoped the buyout wasn't a total disaster.

Swiftly, she dressed with care, choosing a tailored black suit and white silk blouse. She looped and pinned her hair behind her head, gathered her papers and headed for the Holcomb office. Sunshine spilled over traffic and the blue sky and busy street made it seem like any other day, but she knew this day would go down in the history of her family as one of the worst.

She drove to the back to her special parking place, noticing her grandfather's long, black sedan already in his reserved place on the other side of the door, opposite hers.

She entered the brick building for a short meeting before they would meet with Nick and the Ransome people. She closed her eyes, praying swiftly for a miracle to save them, and then went to the meeting to hear the last-ditch efforts of their lawyers and accountants. But if any miracle had occurred, she would have heard about it before now. There was a remote possibility because the attorneys had found a slim chance they could get financing if they could meet certain requirements, but it would take a month or two that they didn't have.

Promptly at fifteen minutes before ten o'clock, she arrived at the Ransome Energy building. She rode up in the elevator with her granddad and their people, but her thoughts were on her first visit to Ransome Energy, when she had asked Nick if they could get together privately.

She had never expected what had resulted. That morning when she had walked into his office, she wouldn't have guessed it possible. When she saw him, her pulse had jumped and she knew with certainty the same reaction would occur today.

She emerged from the elevator, walked down the hall and entered a reception area filled with people, but she didn't see Nick. She guessed that he was still in his office.

"Good morning," she heard a familiar deep voice behind her say, and she turned.

Nine

Nick sauntered toward her and there was no way to stop her physical reaction to him. Her heartbeat quickened and her mouth went dry. Desire burned as hotly as ever and she forgot about any meeting.

How devilishly handsome he looked in his charcoal suit and red tie! His hair was neatly combed, but unruly curls still tangled. Memories of her fingers winding in his thick locks taunted her. In spite of the differences between them, she melted at the sight of him. From the start, she had known that she shouldn't succumb to his charm, but it was too late for regrets now.

Ten minutes into the meeting, Julia realized she was in trouble. For the first time in her life, she couldn't keep her mind on business at hand. Never had she had difficulty concentrating in a meeting, but now all she could think about was Nick, their dinner together tonight, the essential, unbridgeable differences between them. While her thoughts swirled about her personal life, she looked to the end of the table at Nick.

He could turn off everything else. Watching and listening to him, she knew his focus was totally on the matter at hand. When his gaze met hers, his dark eyes were impersonal, unfathomable.

He was cold, ruthlessly efficient and going ahead with his plans in spite of their attorneys' suggestions and offers. Holcomb was vulnerable, and Nick was taking advantage of it to acquire their company.

She knew that was a biased opinion. He was making a savvy business deal and if it hadn't been Holcomb and her family's business, she had to admit that she would agree with what he was doing. He was acquiring rigs for his company that would enlarge his profits enormously. He was making his company stronger, and she reluctantly had to admit he was paying them more than Holcomb was currently worth and a generous sum that few would find complaint with. An amount he didn't have to pay to get what he wanted.

She was hurt and angry and it was difficult to think reasonably or to pay attention to what was happening—a problem she had never had before in her life.

Her grandfather's face was flushed, his fists were clenched and at any minute she expected him to walk out because he couldn't do anything to change the outcome. It was no longer necessary for him to be there, either, because the Holcomb attorneys could handle the details.

"If you'll give us a month more," Rufus said, "we can come up with the money. If you're truly not out for revenge, you'll do this. Tell him, Julia."

She heard her name, but she hadn't heard another word her granddad had spoken. All eyes were on her and her face flushed hotly. She had no idea what had just been said.

"It won't matter what you tell us about holding off for a month," Nick said quietly, letting her know what she had been asked. Embarrassed, she felt foolish, yet business didn't matter right now as much as other aspects of her life. Success was all-important to Nick, also to her grandfather. To her, other facets of her life were far more important. She listened as Nick continued smoothly and again she wondered about him and what he truly felt.

"You win, Nick," her granddad said. "All your life you've been aiming for this moment, and your dad before you. I'm surprised he isn't here to gloat this morning. You've taken advantage of us in every way possible," he snapped, startling Julia.

"It's a fair offer," Nick said quietly.

"You're a shark going in for the kill. Go ahead. Finish me off, but I won't stay and watch." He stood and the others came to their feet. Julia met Nick's cool gaze. She knew there was no point in her staying and listening to them hash out the details.

"I suspect our attorneys can handle the rest. Tyler—" Nick said. His words were clipped and there was no exaltation in the tone of his voice. She followed her grandfather. Nick reached the door before she did and held it open for her. She detected his aftershave as she passed him and it triggered unwanted memories that taunted her.

Her grandfather had already taken the elevator down. She followed and caught up with her grandfather in the lobby. "Granddad! Wait," she called.

"I'm getting out of here," Rufus said, glaring at Nick who emerged from an elevator and approached them.

"I'll see you at home," she said.

When Rufus hurried away, she turned to Nick as he walked up to stand only inches from her.

"You won in every area. You seduced me. You've taken over Holcomb. You've beaten Granddad. You must be planning to celebrate, Nick."

"That wasn't why I made love to you," he declared solemnly, "and you damn well know it. And this buyout is a generous purchase. When the dust settles you and your grandfather will see that you got a profitable bargain."

He took her arm and pulled her closer. "In the meantime, I still want to have dinner together tonight."

The slight contact of his hand on her arm sent her heart racing and she stared up at him, torn by conflicting emotions.

During the past hour, she had hurt for her grandfather and the meeting had been a reminder of how cold and ruthless Nick could be.

At the same time, her heart raced and her breathing suffered and she reacted to Nick merely telling her that he wanted to see her. He wound his fingers in her hair and tilted her head back. Pins and locks of her hair tumbled over his hand, but she didn't care. She slid her hands up his arms, feeling the luxurious soft wool of his sleeves.

"I want you. I want to see you and I want to love you and I know you want me. Don't take us away from each other, Julia," he urged.

Her heart slammed against her ribs. Before she could answer him, the elevator doors behind them opened and Tyler stepped into the lobby. "We want you in the meeting, Nick."

"You'll have to wait," Nick replied. "This is urgent. You take care of it."

Tyler shot her a quizzical look. He left and she heard the door close, but she wasn't thinking about Tyler or watching him.

"I want to come see you and talk to you tonight. All right?" Nick asked.

"No, it's no longer what I want to do," she said, ignoring her racing pulse, trying to keep a barrier of refusal between them. "This evening isn't a good time."

"Julia, I won't give up like this," he declared firmly. He stepped closer and lowered his voice, but she could still hear the urgent note in his tone. "It's too important that I see you. I have to get back to the meeting, but I'd like to see you. How about seven at your place? I'll bring something to eat. Let me come talk to you."

In spite of the emotional upheaval of the morning, she couldn't resist him. "All right. Seven."

"Don't do anything. I'll bring what we need for dinner." As she looked into his dark eyes, she was drawn by the same hot desire she saw in his gaze. People milled in the lobby, but they ceased to exist to her. There was only Nick. Julia tightened her fingers on his arm slightly. Nick inhaled and then he leaned down to place his mouth on hers and kiss her. Torn between wanting to kiss him and wanting to push him away, she lost the battle and returned his kiss.

The moment she did, she forgot the differences between them. She knew each kiss was kindling for a bonfire of wanting Nick. It steadily burned higher and hotter and she wasn't helping herself now.

He straightened, and she opened her eyes. Nick touched her chin. "Seven. Give me a break here. Holcomb got a good deal and if it hadn't been Ransome Energy, it would have been someone else buying you out."

"I know you're right," she admitted.

"I'm glad to hear you agree. Tonight, darlin'," he said, striding away from her.

She watched him with churning emotions while his endearment echoed in her mind, *"...darlin'..."* If only—she thrust the thought out of mind. Nick was who he was and he wasn't going to change because of her.

He got what he had wanted from her, from her family. Yet at the same time, he felt something strongly, too, or he wouldn't make such an effort to see her again.

"He's already breaking my heart," she said softly to herself, knowing she should tell him goodbye tonight. She was in love with him. She hoped it wasn't irrevocable, but at the moment, she felt as if she would love him the rest of her life.

As he stood in front of the elevators, he looked back at her. They stared at each other for a moment before she walked away. She emerged out into hot July sunshine and walked to her car.

She needed to see her grandfather first and then go home. Nick was coming tonight and bringing dinner. The knowledge excited her and she shook her head. "You're hopelessly in love with him," she whispered, "while he's in love with what he's doing up there in that meeting right now."

To her surprise, her grandfather stood beside her car.

"I didn't know you were waiting," she said, rushing to him.

"I figured you'd be worried and hurry over to the house." He gave her a hug. "Don't worry, honey. The dust hasn't settled. We've got money again and a lot of it. We made a large amount of money this morning."

Startled, she stepped back to study him. "You're taking this well," she said.

His blue eyes crackled with anger and his face was still flushed, so she knew he wasn't happy despite his words.

"My family started the drilling company with one wildcat well. We've got money now and I can begin again. There are little companies that we can buy, rigs out there. Nick's young and I've got some years left in me. I can still give him competition and by Jupiter, I intend to!"

"Just don't let your blood pressure go sky high while you think about it and plan, Granddad." She gave him a squeeze and stepped back to look at him. She loved him and didn't want to see him hurt. "We'll meet with our officers and the legal staff this afternoon and map out what we'll do. Maybe Nick will give us some time for the transition."

"Don't count on it," Rufus remarked darkly.

"I'll see you at the office," she said and watched her grandfather stride around to his car. She wished he'd retire and take it easy, but she knew that wasn't his nature. The feud between the two families had just escalated. In spite of it, she was seeing Nick again tonight. She hadn't told her grandfather about seeing Nick, because she expected her relationship with Nick to be brief, over with tonight if she could stick to what she planned.

As she climbed into her car, she glanced back at the building, knowing Nick was doing what he liked best—achieving success in an endeavor he had given years to. Revenge was his today. Success, revenge—how much more important were they to him than love?

Nick stood at a window in a hall and gazed at Julia's car. She hadn't driven away yet and he wondered how hurt she was. Victory over Holcomb was empty, and revenge no longer mattered. He wouldn't back out of the deal because it was a good one for all concerned, whether Rufus saw it that way or not, but there was no satisfaction in smashing Rufus. Not if it hurt Julia.

Nick reminded himself that he would see her this evening. He wanted Julia to move in with him and he would ask her again tonight. He glanced at his watch and decided he would go to a jewelry store and get her a gift. He wanted the day to fly by so it would be time to see her.

"Nick?" Tyler's tone was quizzical and he frowned, studying Nick as he walked up to him. "We're waiting."

"Yeah. Tyler, I want you to offer Rufus a vice presidency with us. We'll absorb his company, but there's room for him."

"You've lost it, Nick! Bringing Rufus in with us is crazy after—"

"Do it, Tyler," Nick ordered flatly in a tone that made Tyler close his mouth. "I think you can handle the meeting from here on. None of you need me. I've already signed the papers I need to sign."

"You're going soft on this deal of acquiring Holcomb! And it's because of Julia. You're in love with her and not using your brain," Tyler snapped, his face flushed. "You worked to demolish that old man and now you want to turn around and offer him a job with us so he can continue with his old projects."

"That's right, Tyler. And it's my prerogative to do all of that," Nick said, pushing his coat open to place his hands on his hips.

"I don't give a damn what you do when you're out of here, but you're making a mistake to offer Holcomb anything. Crush him like you planned. Here's why."

Tyler held out a manila folder. Nick took it and opened it to see the picture of the man running across the Ransome rig in the Gulf. "We've got an identification," Tyler continued. "He's a Holcomb employee."

Nick drew a deep breath and anger stabbed him that Rufus had lied about involvement, but he wasn't surprised. He had known all along that the culprit would turn out to be someone hired by Rufus.

"Rufus knew about it and hired him himself," Tyler said.

"We've got the whole story from another guy who's his friend—in a manner of speaking, since he turned the arsonist in for the reward money. He's friends with this guy and he helped him. We promised anyone who gave us information immunity, so we have to stick with it."

Nick nodded and took the manila folder.

"Now, forget the offer to Rufus and fling that picture at him," Tyler urged. "I'll tell him that we have a confession and know the culprits."

"No. I'll deal with Rufus. Leave this to me. We own his company and all this is over."

"You can't be serious!" Tyler exclaimed. "It's a criminal act."

"It's done. Let it go. Let the guy know that we have evidence and a picture so he won't do it again, but drop it, Tyler," Nick ordered firmly.

"Damn, you really are in love with Julia. Never before in your life would you have made a decision like this."

Startled, Nick stared at his vice president. "I guess I do love her, but it's not the first time I've been in love," he said, knowing when he said the words that they didn't apply to how he felt about Julia. It was the first time he'd felt his way, but he wasn't about to admit the truth to Tyler.

"And she's in love with you," Tyler said with a note of disgust. "She was lost in the meeting. She didn't hear anything we said. Every time the two of you look at each other, the air all but bursts into flames. I'm surprised you lost our bet."

"Well, I did."

"There's always a woman in your life, but this is different," Tyler said and Nick stared at him. "She distracts you from business. That's a first."

"It's none of your business, Tyler," Nick said in a cold voice.

"Dammit, it's my business when you start making bad business calls because of it. You've gone soft and you're gaga over a chick."

"Don't call her a chick. You wind up, Tyler. I have something more important to do," Nick said, turning and walking away. He stopped and faced Tyler again. "Don't show that picture and we're not telling Julia that her grandfather hired the man. The old man lied to her. Just leave it alone. She worships him."

"She's wound you around her little finger. I never thought I'd see the time that a woman had you tied in knots or jumping through hoops."

Nick shrugged. He didn't care what Tyler thought. He just didn't want Julia hurt unnecessarily or disillusioned about her grandfather because there was nothing to gain from it.

He turned his back on Tyler and strode toward the entrance.

"Nick, dammit! You're not thinking straight. Start thinking with your brain. It would have been better if she'd let you seduce her because then you'd have gotten her out of your system."

While Tyler was still ranting, Nick left. Thinking about tonight, he strode outside into hot sunshine. He glanced again at his watch, wishing he could be with Julia right now. He climbed into his car, drove to Holcomb Drilling and was ushered into Rufus's cluttered office.

Rufus stood behind a desk piled high with papers. More papers, ledgers and books were strewn on the floor around the desk. Sunlight spilled through the long windows behind him.

With his blue eyes flashing fire, Rufus glared at Nick. "So you came to gloat. I might have known," Rufus said in disgust.

"No, sir," Nick replied, holding his temper. "I came to tell you that we have a photograph and a witness who is willing to testify that you personally ordered the arson on our rig."

"You're bluffing and wasting my time and yours. There's no such proof or witness."

"I'm telling the truth and you know it," Nick said quietly. "I can produce the photograph, the witness and his sworn statement if I want," Nick said, holding out the manilla folder he carried.

Rufus grabbed the folder from him and opened it, pulling out the photographs of the arsonist running across the Ransome rig. Dropping the pictures on his desk, Rufus looked up. "You bastard!" he snapped, clenching his fists and charging around his desk toward Nick, who stepped back quickly.

"Sir, I won't fight with you," Nick said, holding up both hands, palms toward Rufus in a show of peace.

Suddenly Rufus stopped and all color drained from his face.

Afraid Rufus was having a heart attack, Nick stepped forward to catch him if he collapsed. "Are you all right?" Nick asked.

"You're going to tell Julia," Rufus said, his shoulders slumping. "You're going to destroy me in her eyes and get revenge for everything."

Concerned, Nick shook his head. "No, sir. I'm not going to tell Julia. No charges will be pressed. This matter is between you and me."

"You're lying. I don't believe you," Rufus said, sitting in the closest chair. He trembled and his voice lost its force. Nick's worry increased because Rufus seemed to be aging before his eyes. He looked old, frail and frightened.

"I mean what I say," Nick assured him. "We'll warn your employee never to do it again. That's all. Julia will never know."

With a perplexed expression, Rufus gazed up at Nick. "Why? Why are you backing off when Tyler can finally destroy me and get revenge for all I've done?"

Nick looked down into the blue eyes of the man who had caused him so much trouble through the years. Revenge no longer mattered and he knew why.

"I love Julia," Nick declared quietly, and Rufus flinched as if Nick had struck him. "I want to avoid hurting her."

While Rufus blinked and stared at him, Nick was relieved to see a little color return to Rufus's face. "Are you all right?" Nick asked again.

"Yes. Does she love you?"

"I hope so, sir," Nick said.

Taking a deep breath, Rufus stood. "Don't you ever hurt her."

"I don't intend to," Nick said.

"Now get the hell out," Rufus said, beginning to sound more like the man Nick had always known.

Glad to go, Nick turned and hurried to his car while he thought about what had just passed between Julia's grandfather and him.

As he climbed into his car and made his way to the highway, Nick had forgotten Rufus and was thinking only about Julia. He was in love with her.

He couldn't commit to marriage, which was what she wanted, but he loved her and he wanted her to move in with him. His pulse raced at the thought. She had given him her virginity— a first in his life. It surprised him that it was important to him and made him feel special in her life. He would have never guessed he would feel that way about it, but he did.

She was vital to him and he loved her. More than he had ever loved anyone else.

He entered the flow of traffic and headed for his favorite jeweler. He wanted to buy something for her. Eager to please her and to be with her, he wished the hours would fly past.

"Julia, darlin'," he sighed. "I love you." He needed to tell her that he wanted her to live with him. Would she accept life and love on his terms?

The thought of coming home each night to her built his anticipation. He wanted her in his bed every night. Excitement bubbled in him and he drummed his fingers impatiently on the steering wheel while he thought about holding her close in his arms in his bed tonight. "Julia, Julia," he whispered.

By five o'clock Julia was surprised at the turn her life had taken. Nick had offered to keep Holcomb intact, just absorb it into Ransome Energy. He had offered Rufus a vice presidency in drilling, but her grandfather didn't want to cooperate. It would mean few changes and Holcomb would be part of a profitable larger company and she wanted her grandfather to accept, but he refused to listen.

She drove home at five to get ready to see Nick. Dazed, she entered her house.

Her anger with Nick evaporated earlier. He had mollified her feelings about the bet, made her grandfather an overwhelmingly generous offer. How could she stay angry with him or even think about business? Her usual excitement over seeing Nick was tempered by her resolution to break off with him tonight.

She didn't want to settle down on his terms. Every day she was with him, she was falling deeper in love with him. She wanted everything—not just part of him. And she knew the time had come to tell him.

If they never saw each other again, she would pay that price because she wasn't going to live with him, love him with her whole heart, become accustomed to him in her life and then have him walk away and leave her with only heartbreak.

Solemnly, she dressed in her green silk slacks and green sleeveless blouse. She caught her hair behind her head, tying it with a scarf.

When the doorbell rang, she dashed to open the door. Nick stood patiently waiting and the sight of him took her breath as always. He gave her a glance that held warm approval.

"Are you going to invite me in?" he asked.

In brown slacks and a tan knit shirt, he stood with his hands filled with a sack of food and covered dishes.

"Of course," she said, touching his wrist. "Let me get that." She took a dish from him and carried it to the kitchen.

She was excited. Her resolve to end it with him wavered as it had each day because she wanted to be with him more than anything else she had ever desired in her life. There was no way she could refuse to see him yet. In that moment, she wondered if she would stay and let Nick break her heart.

She turned to face him and he placed his hands on her shoulders. "Still angry with me?"

"No. I was at Granddad's when Tyler called and offered him a place in your business and told him what you were going to do."

"He didn't want any part of it."

"No, but you offered, Nick. That's what mattered to me. I'm not angry and Granddad is busy plotting how he can start up a new company."

"That old pirate!" Nick let out his breath and stared at her. "You're not concerned now about your grandfather. Business is behind us. There's something worrying you and I want to erase it completely. Save it for later. For now, let's have everything I've waited for all day long," he said quietly, running his hands up and down her back. His touch was light, slow and tantalizing. His brown gaze bore into her, and desire consumed her.

"You're wonderful and you're necessary to my existence," he said softly, leaning down to kiss her throat. His words fueled her hot desire. Unable to wait or resist, she stepped into his arms and stood on tiptoe to kiss him passionately; she forgot about dinner or decisions.

With shaking hands, she unfastened his clothes, tugging on him as she led him while they kissed. They got as far as the hall when Nick peeled away the last of her clothes, tossing her lacy panties aside. Desperation shook her and she knelt to take him into her mouth and lick and kiss him while her hands played lightly between his legs.

"Julia, I want you," he ground out the words and picked her up.

"My bedroom," she said hoarsely, waving her hand as he carried her in the direction she had pointed while she wrapped herself around him and kissed him as if this were the last kiss they would ever have.

They fell across her bed. "Nick, protection—" she reminded him. He left her, but return swiftly.

She watched him striding toward her, virile, nude and aroused. Her heartbeat thundered and she slid off the bed, throwing herself into his arms.

He caught her easily as she wrapped her long legs around him and then he placed her in bed again and moved between her legs, pausing to put on a condom. She ran her hands over his thighs, feeling the strong muscles, the hair on his legs.

He lowered himself to thrust into her. "I love you, Julia," he murmured.

She thrilled to his declaration, taking it now without question. "I love you," she whispered in return as she showered his face with kisses. "Love me, Nick. Make love to me all night."

He groaned and slowed, thrusting and then easing back while she thrashed beneath him and pulled him closer. Her legs tightened around him. "I love you, Nick, with all my heart. Absolutely," she said softly, wanting to add *forever,* but refraining because she knew it wouldn't be what he wanted to hear.

As he plunged into her, he kissed her, and they moved together. She stopped thinking, drowning in sensations, aware of his strength and hardness, for a moment feeling as if they both wanted each other with equal urgency and depth.

Release was a starburst, carrying her over the moon. Clinging to him, she cried his name. "Nick!"

He reached a furious climax, his hips thrusting hard as he gasped. "My love!" His words were a husky rasp, but she heard him. He held her tightly and kissed her. Her happiness was a bright, fragile bauble. Her breathing became regular, her heartbeat calm. Wanting to prolong the moment and shut out the problems, she held his damp body close against her. For now, Nick was in her arms; he had told her he loved her, and her heart thudded with joy.

Still holding her close, he shifted, turning on his side. She could feel his heart beating when she ran her hand slowly down the smooth curve of his back. "This is paradise, Nick. It's perfection."

"You're what's perfection," he said in a throaty voice. "I think I should find that furry mutt and give him a home for life and all the bones he can chew. I'll be eternally grateful to him."

She smiled and ran her fingers along Nick's smooth jaw. "You just shaved."

"I planned to see someone special."

"We would have met with or without the dog. You were having dinner with me."

"But if we'd just met at dinner, I wouldn't have felt the same, and neither would you. There was too much animosity steaming through dinner. But out there in the parking lot because of that mutt, we were just two strangers. A man and woman, with chemistry like dynamite between us. No, I owe that mutt, but hopefully he has a home."

"If he has a home, he should have been there instead of wandering in front of speeding cars."

"You always make it sound as if I raced through the parking lot like a criminal."

"Not a criminal, Nick. But you did race. You were in a big rush and I was frightened for the dog because I saw you coming."

"I'm glad I didn't run over you. But you knew you were safe. You knew any man on earth would stop on a dime if you stepped in front of his car."

She smiled at him. "This is good, Nick. This week has been the best in my life."

His eyes darkened as he held her. "It's been the best in mine, too."

"Even if I have missed a few meals."

"So let me see, are you getting too skinny anywhere?" he asked, running his hands over her.

"Nick!" she caught his hands as she laughed. "Speaking of food, I'm getting hungry."

"Very well. First, there's something I want to show you. Promise to sit right where you are and let me get it."

"I promise," she said with a smile.

He slid off the bed and strode from the room to return in seconds. "Close your eyes," he said.

She closed her eyes, wondering what he was doing. She felt the shift of the bed with his weight. "Okay, open your eyes."

He sat in front of her holding out a long, black box. "Nick!" she exclaimed, guessing he had bought her a gift. She opened the lid and looked at a diamond pendant snug against a cream-colored lining.

"Nick, it's beautiful!" she exclaimed.

"Turn around," he said, taking the pendant from her and dropping it over her head before he fastened it. The large diamond was cool against her skin, dazzling in the light. She touched it and was astounded he had gotten it for her.

She turned around, looking into his eyes and feeling as much one with him as she had in the throes of passion and making love to him. "Thank you," she said softly. "I love it, and I'll always treasure it. It's an heirloom, a keeper, Nick, like you." He wrapped her in his arms, sinking down on the bed and leaning over her to kiss her.

He finally raised his head. "It's just a symbol, Julia. My love is as lasting."

She wanted to cry out that he didn't mean what he said, because his love wouldn't last. Instead she kissed him again.

Finally, she pushed against his chest. "Nick, I have to eat. I feel faint," she said.

"Wimp. All right. Point us in the direction of the shower and we'll get ready again for dinner."

"Right through that door and I can walk all by myself."

He stood and reached down to pick her up. "Not while I'm around. You're a feather and I want to carry you. It's a treat to have a gorgeous, naked woman in my arms. There are few things better. Not many, but a few."

"I'm not asking what," she said with amusement. He carried her to the shower to set her on her feet and they showered together.

Afterwards, when they sat in the kitchen alcove to eat tilapia fillets Nick had helped Julia grill, Julia was still torn between what she knew she should do and what she wanted to do.

"Julia," he said, taking her hand in his across the table. "The necklace is a bribe. I want something."

Her pulse jumped and she held her breath. The moment became etched in her memory for all time—Nick in his tan shirt, curly locks of his dark hair falling over his forehead. His chocolate eyes were intent and his expression solemn. She became aware of every detail of the moment—the smell of their steaks, the music playing softly, the flickering candlelight in her quiet kitchen. Her gaze roamed over his features that she now knew so well—his sensual, full underlip, his smooth jaw and strong column of his neck. While her heart drummed, she knew what she hoped he would ask. "What is it, Nick?" she asked quietly, thinking her heartbeat was a drumroll for his announcement.

"Julia, I love you. I want you with me all the time. I want you in my bed every night, in my arms. I was serious today when I asked. Will you move in with me?"

Ten

While her heartbeat raced, his words both thrilled and disappointed her. "Nick, love to you is so casual. 'I love you' rolls easily off your tongue and you've told me that you've been in love lots of times."

"Not like this," he answered solemnly while he ran his thumbs lightly back and forth over her knuckles. "You're different, Julia. I've never wanted a woman like I want you."

Magic words that made her pulse quicken, yet how easily he said them. How many others had he said them to, she wondered. She looked down at their hands together, her fingers wrapped in his while she mulled his offer, knowing it wasn't what she had hoped it would be.

"Nick, where are we going? I move in for how long—a year? A month?"

"You know it'll be longer than a month. Who knows how long? It's good between us and you know it. No one can predict the future. I've told you from the first that I'm not a marrying man," he said, the first note of chill coming into his voice.

"And I made it clear from the first that I am a marrying woman. I want it all, Nick. I want the in-laws, the vows, the permanency. Don't you want kids and a family?"

"Not necessarily. I don't know anything about raising kids, and Matt will have the children in the family."

His request was temptation beyond measure to her. She wanted him, wanted to live with him and love him daily. It could grow into permanency. "Nick, I want you in my life so badly," she said softly.

He took her hand and pulled her on to his lap. "If you're not ready to answer, you think about it, Julia. And let's stay together tonight. I've been waiting all day for this time with you. It's special. Don't take it away from me."

"This is the best!" he said quietly. "You in my arms. That's what I want."

Stay, take another week with him and then break off. Or stay indefinitely and let life unfold. Nick might want her with him so badly, he would ask her to stay forever. She knew she could stay to see if she liked life on his terms. The possibilities danced before her, dazzling in the prospect of being in his arms every night, sharing kisses and passion.

For a few minutes, she gave herself over to thinking about how exciting living with him would be and how much she would like it, but then she faced reality. She couldn't imagine being happy for long when love might be fleeting, and she definitely wanted children.

With sadness, she knew it wouldn't work for her. Their lives were on divergent tracks. She couldn't change and he couldn't change.

She pulled back to look at him. "I'm with you tonight."

He placed his fingers on her mouth. "Whatever your answer. Tell me in the morning. Give me tonight for certain, Julia," he said and she nodded, relief surging in her because it would be one more night with him.

"Very well," she said and held him tightly

That night they loved until dawn streaked the sky. She slept a brief time and woke in his arms. She turned to look at Nick. He was naked, warm, pressed tightly against her with his arm around her. Her hair spilled over his shoulder.

He opened his eyes to look at her. "Good morning," he said in a husky voice that held a note of intimacy. Her pulse raced and she leaned down to kiss him lightly on the mouth.

"Good morning yourself," she replied, tingling as he traced his forefinger over the curves of her breasts.

"Did you think about what I want? Will you move in with me, Julia? It's not far from your house."

"It's a heartbreak away. Nick, I can't. I told you that from the very first," she said.

To her surprise, he winced as if he'd received a blow. Then he drew her into his arms and kissed her passionately. He stopped abruptly and raised his head. "I want you. I need you in my life." Desire burned in his brown eyes and his voice was earnest.

"Nick, I don't want the temporary agreement," she explained, looking into his dark eyes while she felt as if her heart were splintering into a million shards of glass. "I love you. I may love you the rest of my life. Right now, I feel like I will."

"Then, dammit, move in with me. Maybe I'll want to marry after a time. Take a chance here, Julia. Let go your rigid rules."

"It isn't rules. I just think that your way holds much more chance for a dreadful heartbreak whereas now, I think I'll survive."

"You don't have to survive heartbreak," he persisted. "I love you and want you and maybe it'll turn into marriage. Give us a chance."

She hurt badly, wanting him and knowing everything he was telling her might be the best possible solution, but she didn't want to take that chance.

"What about children? You don't want them. I do. That's pretty simple and poles apart."

He inhaled and studied her. "I've never thought of myself in relation to having a family. It's been out from day one, but if you want a child—I'd think about it."

"That's not good enough," she said. "I want a child with the man I love more than I want anything else in life. You don't and that's your choice and you'll be happy with what you've chosen, but I can't change what I feel just so I can live with you and have the pleasure of your company for the next year."

He looked at her and desire blazed in his dark eyes. He tightened his arms and pulled her into his embrace while he kissed her until she shook and her head reeled and she wanted him to the exclusion of every other thought.

She wanted him inside her, wanted his strength and vitality and loving. But their values had come between them. She pushed against his chest.

He leaned away. "Julia—"

She placed her fingers on his lips. "Shh, Nick. Not now. We're on divergent paths, want different things in life. It's been wonderful. I'll give you back your pendant," she said, reaching behind her neck to unfasten the chain.

He caught her hands. "You keep it. I bought it for you and I want you to have it. You want me to walk out of your life, just like that?"

"It hurts to lose you and I think it's going to hurt for a long time, but I have to say goodbye."

"Dammit, Julia! Stop hurting both of us."

"It's a smaller hurt compared to a larger one later on," she said, struggling to hold back tears, letting her gaze roam over him, memorizing the sight of him.

"You don't know that. Give us a chance. I may change and want children. It's something I hadn't ever considered doing. Let me get used to the idea but don't leave me while I do."

"Nick, if you really loved me the way I love you and the way I want to be loved, we wouldn't be having this conversation," she said softly. "'I love you' rolls off your tongue with ease because you're practiced at it, but it's superficial. You don't love in life-and-death, love-forever way. That's what I want."

While silence stretched between them, they stared into each other's eyes. Nick inhaled and turned. "I guess it's time for me to get my things and go." She watched him leave the room.

She brushed back tears, hating that she couldn't control her emotions, hurting and feeling as if her insides were shattering. It was her heart breaking into pieces, she knew. She had loved him in spite of all her logic, common sense and warnings to herself. But who could stop love when it happened and when it was true and special and right?

"Nick," she cried lowly, letting tears fall and wondering how many years it had been since she had shed tears over anything.

She wiped away her tears and walked toward the front as he appeared. A muscle worked in his jaw and he was solemn, gazing intently at her. He crossed the hall to her and placed his hands on her waist. "So you're not giving us a chance? Or giving me a chance?"

"People don't change, Nick."

"They change constantly. I just can't promise anything more right now except that I love you and want you with me. That's a helluva lot, Julia," he added tightly.

Her insides clenched and she hurt. She didn't want him to go because when he went through the door, she knew he wouldn't be back. She flung her arms around his neck to kiss him hard and long.

He leaned over her, thrusting his tongue deep, a kiss that she would remember always. His tongue stroked hers, explored her mouth, firing up desire into fiery need. Suddenly he released her, his dark eyes searching hers.

"If that's what you want," he said. He walked past her, opened the door and strode outside. She couldn't see for a blur of tears. She hurt. She wanted to run to call him back. She felt as if he had yanked her heart out and was carrying it away with him.

But she let him go because she knew what she wanted wasn't what he wanted.

His car motor roared to life. She heard it fade away and then he was gone.

For one of the few times in her adult life, she sobbed. She hurt and she already missed him, and she wondered if she would hurt over him the rest of her life.

* * *

The next week Julia threw herself into her job because the transition would take a month. At present, all Holcomb employees were continuing with their regular tasks. She still worked in their building, but it would close at the end of the month. She had an offer from Nick's company, but the thought of seeing him daily at work was something she didn't want to deal with so, she had started sending out her résumé and making contacts for another job.

Wednesday morning, she stopped at her granddad's. She had never told him about Nick and there was no need to now. He knew something was wrong in her life, but he credited it to the buyout of Holcomb and she hadn't enlightened him about it.

As they sat over cups of coffee, he stared at her with a frown. "You're thinner. Don't take this so hard, honey. We'll get along and we're well fixed."

"I know. I've gotten some good job offers. Henry Banks wants me to work for them."

"Ah, that's good. Is it a good offer?"

"Yes, it is."

"You going to take it?"

"I have to interview with them and I want to take my time. I've signed up to tutor kids with reading two afternoons a week. I'll work my schedule around it."

"Julia, are you seeing Nick Ransome?"

Startled, she shook her head. "No, I'm not. I was, but I'm not any longer. It's over."

Rufus scowled at her. "Has he hurt you?"

"How did you know we've been seeing each other?" she asked, wondering who had told her grandfather and how long ago.

"I just heard you were," Rufus said, and she guessed that one of his friends had seen her out with Nick and told him.

She shrugged. "Well, we aren't anymore and I'm fine."

"No, you're not fine. You don't seem happy and you're losing weight. You're busier and busier, like you're trying to forget something."

"It was my choice, Granddad. Don't worry about it."

"Your not seeing him any longer—it's not because of me, is it?" Rufus asked.

"No!" Julia smiled and patted his hand. "Not at all." Glancing at her watch, she said, "I better go."

"You're getting your schedule solidly booked. Still working out?"

She nodded and stood, carrying her cup to the sink. "Yes, and I have to go now. I'll see you later this week."

"Pretty soon, you won't be able to work me into your busy schedule."

She smiled and hugged him. "Yes, I will. I'll always have time for you." She kissed his cheek and left to drive to work, thinking about her volunteer jobs. No matter how busy she kept, she missed Nick. It was worse than she had dreamed it would be.

She didn't want to eat. She couldn't sleep, no matter how hard she worked out or how many miles a day she ran.

She turned into her parking place and rushed to her office, pulling out ledgers and switching on her computer, trying to concentrate on figures and charts, but seeing dark brown eyes and remembering Nick and wanting him. Was life now so much better without him? She had to be honest with herself—there was nothing better about it.

Nick had transformed her world, making it into a special place. Her life had more zest, more excitement, with Nick in it. What happened each day was more interesting when she discussed it with him. And the hours of lovemaking—she ached for his kisses and his arms around her. She wanted his strong body pressed against hers.

With a groan, she ran her hand through her hair and wondered what she had settled for? An empty life with no children and no Nick? She knew she would never meet a man who excited her like Nick had. It had been a once-in-a-lifetime attraction.

Had she made the biggest mistake of her life? The question plagued her daily, and her longing for Nick increased instead of diminishing. She saw him everywhere she went, only it always turned out to be a stranger. She would glimpse a tall, dark-haired man in a crowd and her pulse would quicken. But when she looked, it would be someone else who really bore little resemblance to Nick.

He was in her thoughts most of the time. She desperately tried whatever she could do to think of other things. Nothing worked. Not going out with friends. Not throwing herself into exercise or work.

Nights were the worst time of all. She couldn't sleep and her big empty bed held too many memories of that last night with Nick. Too clearly, she remembered his strong, lithe body sprawled in her bed after making love. She remembered him crossing the room, naked, aroused, breathtaking.

She groaned and rolled over, getting out of bed and raking her hair away from her face. It had been three weeks and she was going crazy. She hurt, she missed him and she was beginning to wonder if that had been the worst mistake of her life.

She wondered about Nick. Did he even miss her? Had he suffered in the least? Did he have any regrets?

When Nick parted with Julia, he sped away without looking back. He could forget her. In his adult life, he had never had a broken heart, heartache, anyone he couldn't do without in his life. He wasn't going to now. The past was past, and he usually could shrug it away and never think about what might have been.

For the next week he worked in a frenzy, trying to shut out nagging thoughts and memories of Julia. By the week's end, he had to admit to himself that he failed miserably and still missed her. He was making mistakes at work because his mind was elsewhere, something that he had never done before in his life.

He packed and flew to his villa in Cozumel, running several hours a day, swimming, working out, trying to exhaust himself and get his mind off Julia. He did no better there about forgetting her or getting over her than he had at home.

He packed and flew back home, going to work grimly, passing her house each day without a glance, until he found a new route that was longer but disturbed him less.

Three weeks later, he stared out across his desk while he mulled over his life and his future.

Marriage with Julia. It was the first time he had considered it as a possibility. And it made his pulse race to think of her always there for him. Restless, he moved to the window and stood staring at traffic below, but seeing her in his arms. Marry Julia. Babies with Julia. He couldn't imagine. He didn't know kids or anything about them. But Julia in his life permanently—the thought made him feel better than he had since the day he had walked out of her house.

He rubbed his jaw and thought about his future. He didn't want to go out with another woman. He wanted Julia only. He had never felt this way in his life. From the very first meeting, everything with Julia had been different, an attraction that bound his heart with golden chains.

Business no longer mattered, and he was beginning to see what she was talking about when she said success wasn't everything. It wasn't anything without her.

"Nick?" Tyler said from the doorway.

"Yes?" Nick turned to stare at Tyler, trying to focus on him and get his thoughts off Julia.

"Do you have the letter you were going to send to Consolidated?"

"Consolidated?" Nick's mind went blank. He inhaled and shook his head. "Refresh my memory."

Frowning, Tyler came into the room and closed the door. "I don't know what's the matter with you—well, yes, I do. Dammit, Nick, go back to Mexico or call Julia Holcomb. You're going to hell in a handbasket here, and you'll take the company with you if you don't watch out."

"Sorry, Tyler. I may take a few days off."

"Take a month. I'll take care of things," Tyler said in a strained tone. "Dammit, go find another woman. Want me to introduce you to someone tonight? Someone that can take your mind off Julia?"

"No, but thanks," Nick answered. "I'll get that letter."

"Let me write it. No telling what you'd put in it," Tyler said darkly.

"You write it. I'm leaving the office."

Tyler nodded and stomped out, slamming the door behind him.

Nick rubbed his neck and glanced at his watch and thought about what he would like to do. He closed his computer and strode out, telling his secretary that he would check back with her, but he would be out of touch for a while and to let Tyler handle everything.

While his heart raced, he pulled out his cell phone to call Julia. Disappointment filled him when she didn't answer. Nor did he get a machine where he could leave a message. Annoyed, he broke the connection and climbed into his car, driving out of the lot and forgetting about the office immediately.

Nick ran errands and periodically tried to call Julia, but no answer. When he drove home, he passed her house, but he couldn't tell whether anyone was home or not. He sped up his drive and parked, striding into the house to strip and shower, his pulse humming. He intended to call her and see her. It was just a matter of time until he got in touch with her.

He dressed in navy slacks and a navy knit shirt. Whistling, on edge and wondering where she was, he tried again to call her.

He heard a car coming up the drive and went striding down to the door. Salesmen weren't allowed in the area, and his family never came without calling.

The engine stopped outside and he heard a car door slam. He went to the door and swung it wide. His heart thudded as he stared at Julia.

In the shade of his porch, the late-afternoon sunlight caught golden highlights in her hair. She looked pale and thinner. Her blue eyes were enormous as she gazed at him.

His insides clutched tightly. "Julia?"

Eleven

When Nick swung open the door, Julia's heart skipped a beat and words failed her. He was a darker tan, fit, so handsome he took her breath.

"Julia?" he repeated. "Come in. I tried to call you."

She stepped inside his quiet entryway, oblivious to her surroundings, seeing only Nick. Her heart pounded and she could only stare at him. "You called me?" she asked, wondering if she had heard correctly above the pounding of her heart. It had been a full three weeks and for all she knew, there could be someone else in Nick's life now. Solemnly, she gazed at him.

They stared at each other, sparks dancing between them. She wanted him as she had never wanted anyone or dreamed she could want someone.

"I was wrong," she said, the words tumbling out quickly. "I want you in my life whatever way I can."

He looked as if she had knocked the breath out of him. He rocked back and blinked. Then he closed the space between them, taking her in his arms to kiss her.

The minute his mouth covered hers and his tongue thrust into her mouth, she knew what he wanted. There was no question of his desire, no doubt he had missed her as much as she had missed him.

"Nick!" she cried, flinging her arms around his neck and kissing him with a hungry desperation that matched his own. He leaned over her, his tongue stroking hers while his hands slid all over her as if he were reassuring himself that she was really there.

She tugged free his buttons and they undressed each other frantically. Nick shook as much as she did.

"It's been forever," she whispered, her hands playing over his strong, naked body. "I'm on the Pill now—" she said softly and then words were gone as he lowered her to the floor and moved between her legs.

"You're my love, Julia," he rasped the words and thrust into her. She wrapped her legs around him, holding him fiercely, moving with him while joy filled her. Nick was in her arms and he wanted her!

Their lovemaking was frantic and when release came, she held him tightly.

"I love you, darlin'," he choked out. Sweat beaded his brow, and he thrust fast and hard, carrying her to a second climax.

"Ah, darlin'." She came down from over the moon, floating in ecstasy, her rapture complete in the knowledge that he wanted her as badly as she wanted him.

"Nick, I missed you," she said, showering kisses on his face, biting his shoulder lightly, running her hands over him as if she still couldn't believe that he was in her arms.

"You couldn't have missed me as much as I did you," Nick protested, drawing his fingers along her cheek. Their breathing was ragged, and she could still feel his heart pounding. "I've thought about you constantly," he said.

His words thrilled her and she buried her face against his throat, breathing the scent of him, relishing every inch of him. "Nick, Nick," she said, over and over, delirious with joy to be in his arms and be able to love him again.

He turned on his side, taking her with him. He glanced around. "We're on the marble floor. Next time, I promise a bed."

"Don't make promises you can't keep. Next time may be in your shower," she said lightly, feeling giddy with happiness. "And I know we're on a marble floor. Now I know it—I didn't until a few seconds ago."

"You were my cushion," he said, stroking her hair away from her face and tucking strands behind her ear.

She framed his face with her hand. "I was wrong, Nick. I can't get along without you. My life was empty and lonely and dreadful without you in it. I'll move in with you if you want me."

"Ah, darlin', if I want you. I don't want to let go of you at all. Let's go see about that shower and whatever else we can do. I'm not sure my knees will work yet, but I'll try."

"You feel as if you've been working out big-time," she said, running her hands down his arms.

"I have," he said, standing and lifting her in his arms easily. "I swim, I jog, I ride, I've done everything I can to exhaust myself and to try to forget you for a few minutes each day."

"Have you really?" she asked, amazed by his declaration.

"Don't act so surprised," he said. "You left a void in my life that was enormous."

"I find that difficult to believe," she said. "At least the last part. You must have been working out to take the stairs the way you just did."

He set her down in his shower and turned warm water over both of them. They showered and dried each other. He drew the towel slowly over her, inching his way down her backside and then just as leisurely down her front.

"Nick!" she gasped, winding her fingers in his hair.

"We just set a record for fast. Now we'll try to set one for slow," he said, nuzzling her throat and moving slowly down her body.

They made love leisurely, moving to the bedroom, loving in his big bed.

Afterwards, they held each other tightly.

"We shouldn't have waited so long," she whispered. "I've been miserable."

He propped himself up to look down at her while she pulled the sheet up beneath her arms. "You'll move in with me?" he asked, watching her closely.

She placed her hand against his face. "Yes, I will. Life was nothing without you, Nick," she said solemnly. Something flickered in the depths of his eyes before he leaned down to kiss her for a long time, a kiss of satisfaction and union.

When he raised his head, he stood. "Don't go away," he said, and turned to cross the room to his dresser.

She watched him, her gaze drifting over his nude body that was superbly fit. "You were sexy and had muscles before. Now you really do."

"I glad you like what you see because it's yours." He sat beside her and pulled the sheet across his hips. "I missed you more than you could possibly have missed me. You said you were wrong. I was the one who was wrong, Julia," he said solemnly and her breath caught.

"I thought about life without you, about marriage, about children. I don't know anything about children, so that's a blank, but I don't want life without you. I want to marry you. Will you marry me?"

Stunned, joy filled her and she gasped, crying out and throwing her arms around his neck, knocking him off balance. She shrieked as they tumbled to the floor and she fell on top of him. Laughing, they rolled over. "Yes! Yes, I'll marry you!" she cried, hugging his neck and then kissing him hard.

In minutes, he sat up while she wriggled to sit on the floor facing him. She yanked the sheet up beneath her arms and gazed into his warm, brown eyes. "You will marry me?" he asked again.

"Yes, Nick, I'll marry you," she replied, happiness keeping her from sitting still as she wriggled and bounced slightly. He took her hand and hunted around on the floor, picked up a ring and slid it on her finger.

She gasped at the sight of the huge diamond that sparkled and caught the light. "Nick! It's gorgeous! It's fantastic!"

"Good. I'm glad you like it," he said with satisfaction.

She tore her attention from her ring to look at him and placed her hand against his cheek again. "You're sure that you want marriage?"

"Positively. I was the one who was wrong, Julia. I want it permanent. I don't ever want to be without you and your love."

"We can have children?" she asked cautiously.

"As many as you want," he said.

"Oh, Nick!" Sliding into his lap, she wrapped her arms around his neck as she let out a sigh. "This is the best day of my life."

"It'll just get better," he said, brushing kisses on her temple.

"I'll have to tell Granddad. Someone told him we were seeing each other. And your family—your father will hate me."

"No, he won't. Once you're in our family, you'll be a Ransome and he'll like you. Now your granddad is another matter. If those two old coots don't want to come to our wedding, I don't care."

"Granddad will come. He'll walk down the aisle with me."

"You want a big wedding?"

"Yes! I want the world to come! Actually, not that big."

"How long is this going to take, Julia? I want to get married tomorrow."

She grinned at him, feeling giddy still. "I can do the whole thing in a month."

"A month!" He groaned. "I don't want to wait."

"You can wait that long and part of the time, I'll be right here, waiting with you," she said, wiggling her hand and looking at her dazzling ring. She smiled at him and ran her fingers through his thick curls. "It's gorgeous, Nick! I never dreamed this was possible."

"Whatever you want, sweetie," he drawled, running his finger across the top of the sheet and over the full curve of her breasts. "I love you, Julia. I want you always."

"Thank goodness, you do! Let's go tell our families and plan this wedding."

He grinned and shook his head as she stood, tugged on his wrist and reached for the phone.

Epilogue

The last week of August, Julia dressed with care, her heart beating eagerly as she smoothed the white satin skirt over her hips. Katherine shook Julia's train and shifted the veil. Katherine was a bridesmaid and wore a simple red dress with a long skirt and spaghetti straps. "You look beautiful," Katherine said solemnly.

Julia gazed at her reflection, unable to believe the day had finally arrived. Her engagement ring caught reflections of light, sparkling as she moved her hands.

"You do look gorgeous," Olivia said. Her red dress was identical to Katherine's.

"Everyone looks beautiful," the tall, black-haired wedding planner said, beaming at them and smoothing Olivia's skirt.

"I can't believe both my brothers will be married," Katherine remarked. "Somehow, I never expected it from Nick, but I'm glad. He'll be a nicer person."

"I think so," Julia said, laughing and feeling giddy. Her pulse skipped and raced with excitement. Tingles danced in her and she couldn't stop smiling. She also couldn't wait to see Nick and was glad they were having a morning wedding.

"It's time to go," the wedding planner said, and the brides-maids went out ahead of Julia. She had three friends who were attendants, plus Olivia and Katherine who would soon be in-laws. Her granddad met her in the foyer and she smiled at him. She paused to straighten his tie and the photographer took their picture.

"How handsome you look!" she exclaimed.

"Hmmph! I probably should be packing with that scoundrel Duke Ransome here."

"Granddad, you promised!" Julia said, giving him a harsh look.

He clamped his mouth shut. "I'll remember and be nice to the Ransomes, although how you could marry one, I don't know."

"I hope you give Nick a chance," she said lightly. "Ready?"

He looked at her and placed his hands on her shoulders. "You're lovely, Julia. All grown up and a beautiful woman. I wish your momma and daddy could see you. And your grandmomma."

"I know," she said quietly. She brushed a kiss on his cheek. "At least I have you."

"Time, Miss Holcomb," the wedding planner said.

Julia turned and linked her arm through her grandfather's. She waited to begin, but already her gaze had gone to the tall, handsome man who waited at the altar and who was watching her now.

The moment she met his gaze, her heart leaped. Joy filled her and she couldn't wait to walk down the aisle, repeat vows and become his wife.

Then they were moving, walking past guests and flowers and garlands, but all she could see was Nick and his dark eyes on her. She might as well have been alone with him. Love for him filled her, and she felt as if she were the luckiest woman on earth that morning.

Her grandfather placed her hand in Nick's warm hand. Nick smiled at her and she smiled in turn. "I love you," she silently mouthed the words to him and he winked at her.

Then they turned to repeat their vows. She stood in a dream world, only it was real—she was actually going to be Nick's wife in minutes.

"I now declare you man and wife," the minister finally announced, introducing them to the guests as Mr. and Mrs. Nicholas Ransome.

"You may kiss the bride."

She turned to Nick, who raised her veil and placed his hand lightly on her waist. His brown eyes were warm with love, and her happiness bubbled in her. When he leaned down to kiss her lightly, his lips were a warm promise. "I love you," he whispered. "You've made me the happiest man on earth today," he said.

"Nick, it's fabulous!" she exclaimed, smiling at him.

Taking her arm, he walked up the aisle beside her. As she passed him, she glanced into Duke's cold blue eyes and wondered if she would ever win over Nick's father. Then the thought was gone, and she didn't care. She couldn't worry about him when Nick kept repeating he loved her.

With a fanfare of trumpets, they rushed up the aisle and into the narthex. Immediately, friends showered them with congratulations until Nick led her through a door. "We have to go back around for pictures," he said, leading her through another door.

"I don't think you're going the way they told us to," she said. He entered a small office and closed the door.

"I'm sure as hell not. I wanted you to myself for a minute," he said, pulling her into his arms, bending over her until she had to cling to his shoulders as she was almost off her feet. His love poured into his kiss while she held him and kissed him in return.

Finally she pulled away slightly. "Let me up, Nick! They'll be searching all over for us and I'll be all rumpled."

He laughed and swung her up. "I can't wait to get you alone and peel you out of everything. I want you naked in my arms for the entire honeymoon!"

She wiggled her hips. "Just you wait," she purred seductively. "I'll make you want to keep your clothes off for the honeymoon, too."

He inhaled and his smile vanished, fires of longing flashing in the depths of his brown eyes. "Dammit, Julia, do you know what you're doing to me!" he growled reaching for her.

With an impish grin, she dodged his grasp. "We better go, Mr. Ransome, so you can get your picture taken with your new wife who can't wait to get your pants off."

"Julia!"

Laughing, she opened the door and stepped into the hall. "Now where do we go to get to the front of the church for pictures."

"You bawdy wench!" Nick growled and turned her to kiss her passionately until she pushed against him.

"Now you've done it! Look at my veil."

He straightened it. "You asked for that kiss."

"I most certainly did not, but we're going to be late—"

"Nick!" came a call.

"That's Katherine. C'mon," Nick said taking her hand.

They posed for pictures and then left for the reception at a country club. A band played, tables were laden with food and the room was filled with the scent of garlands of white roses that decorated the large reception room. From the moment they arrived, Nick and Julia were besieged by well-wishing friends.

Later, Nick led Julia onto the dance floor for the first dance. "Don't be surprised if my father wants a dance."

"I'll faint in shock. He is glaring arrows through me."

"No. He'll change. You're in the family now. Just like Olivia. He tried to buy her off to keep her from marrying Matt."

"No!" Julia exclaimed, realizing where Nick might have gotten his ruthless streak.

Nick nodded. "Matt told me. My dad will go to great lengths to get what he wants."

"I'm not saying anything bad about anybody on this very special day in our lives. Nick, I love you," she said. "You're going to have to get used to hearing me say that over and over."

"I'll never hear it too much," he answered solemnly. "It scares me when I think I almost lost you. If you'd met someone else and fallen in love—"

"That was impossible, so forget it. I was already madly, madly in love with you."

"Good thing," he said, swirling her around on the dance floor. As the number ended, Nick looked over her head. "Here comes my brother."

"Will you give up your bride for one dance with her new brother-in-law?" Matt asked and, without waiting for Nick's answer, looked at Julia. "May I have this dance, sis?"

She laughed and took his hand. As they danced away from Nick, she looked up at Matt. "'Sis.' That sounds wonderful. I'm an only child. I've always longed for a family and finally, now I have one."

"You'll be good for Nick. I've never seen him this relaxed and happy."

"Your dad, on the other hand, wishes the ground would swallow me."

"He'll come around, maybe faster than your grandfather who hasn't shaken hands with any of us yet."

"He hasn't?" she asked, surprised after her lecture to her grandfather.

"Uh-oh. Shouldn't have told you. Don't go fuss at him. He doesn't have to be buddies with us."

"No, but he needs to be civil."

"Leave him alone. We'll all get along. And Dad will thaw. He always does. Watch him with Olivia. He wouldn't speak to her when we married."

"You'd never know it now," Julia said, thinking how she had seen Duke Ransome talking to Olivia often during the wedding activities.

"That's because she has the first Ransome grandbaby. Now he's as good as he can be to her. He comes by the house with baby presents, built a nursery in his house. He can do an about-face before you know it. Now on another subject, I hope you're happy, Julia. I know Nick is."

"I'm deliriously happy. I love him with all my heart."

"Good." Matt spun her around and they danced easily together. The minute the music stopped, she turned to face her grandfather.

"My turn next," he said, nodding at Matt.

She stepped into his arms and danced, and then Nick claimed her. "I know we have to stay for a couple of hours, but then we're out of here."

"Sounds fine to me," she replied, looking up at her handsome husband and wanting to be alone with him.

She drifted through the reception in euphoria, constantly looking at Nick when he was away from her, touching him if he stood close. Joy bubbled in her and she knew she would remember this day all her life.

It was three hours before Nick appeared at her side and took her hand.

"Now's the time, Mrs. Ransome. We're making a break for it. Don't stop for anything."

"Nick. I need to change and we need to tell the family goodbye."

"I told everyone for both of us except your grandfather. We can catch him on the way out, and you leave in your wedding dress. You can change later."

"I have a gorgeous dress in the dressing room."

"I'm sure you do and after we get back from our honeymoon, I'll really appreciate it when I take you out, but right now, we're going to escape. That means we run just as we are. The limo is ready and waiting."

"Nick, we can't—"

"Yes, we can," he said, taking a tighter grip on her hand. "Let's tell Granddad goodbye."

Laughing, she hurried with him to kiss her grandfather. Then they went out through the kitchen and into a delivery area behind. A white stretch limo waited, and a chauffeur opened the door. She climbed in, dropping into a seat and laughing as Nick climbed in and sat beside her.

In minutes, they were moving through traffic. "A perfect getaway."

"Now where are we going?" she asked. "You said you had a surprise."

"How's the Plaza in New York and then on to a villa on the Mediterranean?"

"Fabulous," she said, running her hand along his thigh and swinging her legs across his. "I'll never see any of it."

"You will when we go back on our anniversaries," he said as he wrapped his arms around her and leaned forward to kiss her. He slid his hand down the neck of her dress, caressing her breast until she grasped his wrist.

"Nick, we're not alone here."

"We can be, almost," he said, closing the partition between them and the chauffeur. He turned back to kiss her and she wrapped her arms around his neck.

"I'm not sure I can wait until we get to New York," she said softly.

"You're not going to have to. Tonight is the bridal suite at the Fairmont in Dallas only a short drive away from the country club."

"Why, bless you, Mr. Ransome!" she drawled in a throaty voice. "You do think of everything."

He laughed and tightened his arm around her waist. "It's going to be wonderful, Julia."

"It is, Nick."

Just as he promised, they reached the hotel in a short time. She was aware of heads turning as they crossed the lobby to the elevators. "Everyone is staring at us."

"No, they're drooling over you. The women are thinking how beautiful you are and I don't want to tell you what the men are thinking, but I'm getting you out of here as fast as I possibly can."

Laughing, she walked closely beside him as they followed a bellhop to their suite on the top floor. As soon as they were alone and the door closed behind them, Nick reached to pull her into his arms.

"Welcome home, Mrs. Ransome."

"I love you, Nick. This has been the most wonderful day of my life."

"I want to try to make it the most wonderful night," he said softly, trailing kisses along her throat as he carefully unfastened her veil and tossed it on a chair while he kissed her. His kiss was reassurance, satisfaction, promises, as seductive as ever. She kissed him in return as her heart pounded with joy.

Standing on her toes, she kicked off her shoes and wrapped one arm around his neck while she unfastened his shirt with her other hand. "I love you, love you," she whispered, embracing her tall, handsome husband. Her joy was complete. "Life will be good, Nick," she said and kissed away his answer.

* * * * *

Don't miss Katherine Ransome's story,
SCANDALS FROM THE THIRD BRIDE,
available in November 2006 from Sara Orwig
and Silhouette Desire.

Run, Ally! Don't be fooled by him. He's evil. Don't let him touch you!

But as the forbidding figure came through the mists toward her, Ally knew she couldn't run. His features burned with dark malevolence, and his physical domination of everything around him seemed to hold her like a net.

She'd heard the tales. She knew all about the Wolverton legend and the ghost that haunted The Willows, an elegant old mansion lost by Micha Wolverton nearly a hundred years ago. According to folklore, the estate was stolen from the Wolvertons, and Micha was killed, trying to reclaim it. His dying vow was to be reunited with the spirit of his beloved wife, who'd taken her life for reasons no one would speak of, except in whispers. But Ally had never put much stock in the fantasy. She didn't believe in ghosts.

Until now—

She still didn't understand what was happening. The figure had materialized out of the mist that lay thick on the damp netery soil. A cool breeze and silvery moonlight had played against the ancient stone of the crypts surrounding her, until they joined the mist, causing his body to thicken and solidify right before her eyes. That was when she realized she'd seen this man before. Or thought she had, at least.

His face was familiar…so familiar, yet she couldn't put it together. Not with him looming so near. She stepped back as he approached.

"Don't be afraid," he said. His voice wasn't what she expected. It didn't sound as if it were coming from beyond the grave. It was deep and sensual. Commanding.

"Who are you?" she managed.

"You should know. You summoned me."

"No, I didn't." She had no idea what he was talking about. Two minutes ago, she'd been crouching behind a moss-covered crypt, spying on the mansion that had once been The Willows, but was now Club Casablanca. And then this—

If he was Micah, he might be angry that she was trespassing on his property. "I'll go," she said. "I won't come back. I promise."

"You're not going anywhere."

Words snagged in her throat. "Wh-why not? What do you want?"

"If I wanted something, Ally, I'd take it. This is about need."

His words resonated as he moved within inches of her. She tried to back away, but her feet were useless. "And you need something from me?"

"Good guess." His tone burned with irony. "I need lips, soft and surrendered, a body limp with desire."

"My lips, my bod—?"

"Only yours."

"Why? Why me?" This couldn't be Micha. He didn't want any woman but Rose. He'd died trying to get back to her.

"Because you want that, too," he said.

Wanted what? A ghost of her own? She'd always found the legend impossibly romantic, but how could he have known that?

How could he know anything about her? Besides, she'd sworn off inappropriate men, and what could be more inappropriate than a ghost? She shook her head again, still not willing to admit the truth. But her heart wouldn't play along. It clattered inside her chest. The mere thought of his kiss, his touch, terrified her. This wildness, it was fear, wasn't it?

When his fingertips touched her cheek, she flinched, expecting his flesh to be cold, lifeless. It was anything but that. His skin was smooth and hot, gentle, yet demanding. And while his dark brown eyes were filled with mystery and wonder, there was a sensitivity about them that threatened to disarm her if she looked too deeply.

"These lips are mine," he said, as if stating a universal fact that she was helpless to avoid. In truth, it was just that. She couldn't stop him.

And she didn't want to.

Find out how the story unfolds in...
DECADENT
by
New York Times *bestselling author*
Suzanne Forster.
On sale November 2006.

Harlequin Blaze—
Your ultimate destination for red-hot reads.
With six titles every month, you'll never guess
what you'll discover under the covers...

REQUEST YOUR FREE BOOKS!

2 FREE NOVELS PLUS 2 FREE GIFTS!

Passionate, Powerful, Provocative!

SDES06

SAVE UP TO $30! SIGN UP TODAY

INSIDE *Romance*

The complete guide to your favorite
Harlequin®, Silhouette® and Love Inspired® books.

✓ Newsletter ABSOLUTELY FREE! No purchase necessary.

✓ Valuable coupons for future purchases of Harlequin, Silhouette and Love Inspired books in every issue!

✓ Special excerpts & previews in each issue. Learn about all the hottest titles before they arrive in stores.

✓ No hassle—mailed directly to your door!

✓ Comes complete with a handy shopping checklist so you won't miss out on any titles.

- -

SIGN ME UP TO RECEIVE INSIDE ROMANCE ABSOLUTELY FREE

(Please print clearly)

Name

Address

| City/Town | State/Province | Zip/Postal Code |

COMING NEXT MONTH

#1759 THE EXPECTANT EXECUTIVE—Kathie DeNosky
The Elliotts
An Elliott heiress's unexpected pregnancy is the subject of high-society gossip. Wait till the baby's father finds out!

#1760 THE SUBSTITUTE MILLIONAIRE—Susan Mallery
The Million Dollar Catch
What is a billionaire to do when he discovers the woman he's been hiding his true identity from is carrying his child?

#1761 BEDDED *THEN* WED—Heidi Betts
Marrying his neighbor's daughter is supposed to be merely a business transaction...until he finds himself falling for his convenient wife.

#1762 SCANDALS FROM THE THIRD BRIDE—
Sara Orwig
The Wealthy Ransomes
Bought by the highest bidder, a bachelorette has no recourse but to spend the evening with the man who once left her at the altar.

#1763 THE PREGNANCY NEGOTIATION—Kristi Gold
She is desperate to get pregnant. And her playboy neighbor is just the right man for the job.

#1764 HOLIDAY CONFESSIONS—
Anne Marie Winston
True love may be blind...but can it withstand the lies between them?

SDCNM1006